SEARCHING FOR KEELEY

JULIA BRIGHT

BLURB

Keeley Anderson may not have exactly the life she wants, but she's happy working as a dental assistant. Nothing amazing happens until her boss makes a bad business decision and she's abducted by an organized crime gang hellbent on using her to get money.

FBI agent Noah Grey is tasked with ending the stream of drugs brought into Texas through the many waterways along the coast. When the cute dental assistant he is dating is abducted, he finds he is useless against the wave of crime swamping Texas.

Once Keeley is found, everyone thinks the danger is over, but she knows too much about the thugs' operation, and they come after her.

Noah does the only thing he can think of, spirit Keeley away to a private cabin nestled in the wood of East Texas. Once there, Keeley can't ignore the desire she feels for Noah. But are they safe, or will the crew that took Keeley find them?

CHAPTER ONE

THE ENGINE GRUMBLED AND SPUTTERED ON KEELEY'S old Kia Sportage as she pulled into the parking lot. It jerked to a stop in a spot—thank goodness—and coughed before it died. *Just great.* She'd owned this car since before college, which was before her dad went bankrupt, and before all the trouble happened which made her drop out of Columbia University in New York and move home to San Antonio, Texas.

Though Keeley wished things had turned out differently, she wasn't angry about leaving the art history program, at least not like she used to be. She was glad she'd given it up. Just thinking about the stress of completing her master's degree made her shudder. No way she wanted that. She hadn't wanted to work in a museum, not really. Dreams for the future were for children, and she wasn't a child anymore, her parents had seen to it.

The truth wiggled up, worming its way into her chest, making her ache, but she pushed it away. She had to repel those thoughts of art history or the ache in her heart would rule. Besides, she enjoyed working for Doc Julian as a dental assistant for the most part. It wasn't like she hated her job; she just didn't love it.

Now her car was dead, the rain was falling like crazy, and she had to get inside the building so she could call the first appointment for the day and tell them everyone was running late because of the wrecks on the interstate. Lucky for her, she lived close to the office.

There was a partial break in the rain, and she jumped out of the car, slamming the door shut. Of course, the rain picked up after she took two steps, soaking her before she made it to the covered walkway. She raced up the stairs, using her key to enter the office. She'd just punched in the code for the alarm when lightning struck nearby, cutting the power to the building.

The front door opened and a huge guy stepped in, his face blocked by his big, black dripping wet umbrella.

Fear struck, and Keeley wanted to scream, but just before she let loose a yell to top all yells, the guy lifted his umbrella and flashed her a brilliant smile.

"Wow, it's coming down." His voice was rich and smooth. He had an accent she couldn't place. He wasn't from around here, she didn't think. "I have an appointment. I'm a little early."

"Um, the electricity is out." Why had she said that? She sounded stupid. "Why are you here?" slipped out before she could stop herself. Again, she'd said something dumb.

She dropped her keys and bent to pick them up, spilling the water in her tumbler.

"Oh shit." Her head whipped up as panic flared. "I'm so sorry. You took me by surprise coming in right after lightning struck. I swore no one was in the parking lot when I pulled up."

His lips stretched into a smile as he folded his umbrella, leaning it against the wall. "It's that kind of morning, huh? I've had those too. Let me help you clean up the water."

She shook her head. "No, that's not necessary. I just—" Her keys flew from her hand again, and she dropped her bag, which had a tub of blueberries in the top. The container fell and bounced on the ground then popped open, blueberries rolling all over the area rug that had too much white that would hold stains forever if one of those little round blue bombs burst.

"Oh God," she exclaimed. "Don't step on those. They're blueberries. He'll kill me if they stain the rug."

The dude lifted his eyebrows as he stared at her. She was acting like an idiot. Normal people didn't do stupid stuff like she did. And he happened to be cute, which of course meant she had no hope of recovering.

"I'm Noah, by the way." The guy pulled out his phone and turned on his flashlight. "I'll get the rogue blueberries for you."

"Keeley is my name, but you don't—"

He lifted a hand and shot her a smile. "I know. I'll help anyway."

"Thank you."

This day was terrible and getting worse. Her car was dead, how dead she didn't know, her boss was late, and the electricity was out. She went behind the main desk and put down her bag in her cubby then found something to clean up the spilled water. By the time she mopped it up, Noah had rescued the blueberries. Too bad they'd fallen on the floor. She guessed she could wash them and eat them anyway since they were so expensive. Could she clean the berries enough to make them edible?

She took the tub from him and carried it back to her

cubby, inspecting the fruit through the clear plastic. It probably wouldn't be too bad if she ran them under water.

She moved behind the reception desk and looked at the appointment book. Sure enough, Noah Grey was on the books to see Doc Julian this morning. She glanced up and swallowed as the man moved closer. His blue eyes were mesmerizing, and they seemed to search her soul with an intensity she'd never experienced. It wasn't weird; instead, his gaze was so freaking sexy that it nearly made her shiver.

"I...um, Doc is running late. The wrecks."

Noah grimaced. "Yes, I heard about those." He pulled out his phone, and his lips twisted up on one side. "I guess — "

Suddenly his phone beeped and scared the crap out of her. He jumped too before he silenced the device. His gaze whipped up, and his lips turned down.

"There's a tornado on Fredericksburg at Wurzbach."

His words sent a spike of panic through her. "Oh God. That's right where we are."

"Closet, or bathroom?"

"Closet." She waved him around the desk and headed down the hall. "Doc Julian loves natural light, even the bathroom has a window. All we have is this small closet."

The rain slowed, but the wind picked up. They both looked out the window, seeing scraps of paper and plastic bags swirling in the air. It seemed almost fake, like something she'd seen in a movie about tornados, but this was real.

"It's right here. We don't have a choice," Noah said.

He tugged open the door to the closet and stepped in. It was a tight fit. Doc Julian knew he didn't have a safe space during a storm, but it hadn't been an issue until now.

Noah closed the door, leaving them in the dark as the wind and rain battered the building. Something crashed against the roof, sending her jumping into Noah. He wrapped his arm around her shoulder and pulled her close.

"It'll be fine." Noah's voice was strong and comforted her.

Another crash sounded. Keeley clenched his shirt in her fingers, twisting the fabric. "Sorry, I'm wrinkling your shirt."

"Doesn't matter. I have more at the office."

She glanced up, not able to see anything, but she felt the soft puff of his breath on her cheek. His hands adjusted on her back, and he stepped closer. She drew in a breath, trying to hide the fact she was sniffing him. He smelled of soap and laundry freshener along with mouthwash and a hint of coffee. She liked the uncomplicated scent. Sometimes people came in for work on their teeth, and they smelled like they'd used half their bottle of perfume or cologne. Noah smelled nice, like the type of guy she'd like to date.

Another crash sounded, and Noah's arms tightened around her. She closed her eyes and rested her head against his chest, flinching when something else slammed into the building.

Her heart sped up. "It sounds awful."

"It does." Noah's words floated around the small closet. Another bang made them both jump. "You live here long?"

"Yes, my whole life, except when I left for..." She trailed off, not wanting to talk about school and everything that happened with her dad.

He waited a few seconds before he began speaking. "I moved here a few months ago. Before that, I was in Florida.

We had a few hurricanes while I was there. I've lived in Virginia and my favorite, New York City, well, it was my favorite at the time because I was young and enjoyed the parties and just hanging out."

She sighed wistfully, wishing she'd stayed in New York and finished school. Another crash sounded, and she let go of his shirt and wrapped her arms around his body, holding tight.

"You ever been?" Noah asked.

"What?" She'd forgotten the context as fear had pummeled her.

"To New York."

"Oh, um, yes. I...I went to Columbia for a few semesters."

"Nice, I got my master's in criminal justice at Columbia."

Another crash sounded, this one louder. "That's great. What do you do?"

"I'm an FBI agent."

"Really? That's odd, well I guess it isn't really odd, but it's different. I don't know any agents, or if I do, I don't know that they are agents. Of course, the patients don't talk much because of the stuff in their mouth. It's hard to hold a conversation, rather one-sided. Doc Julian talks a lot, and I guess I do too. I'm usually never in a closet pressed up against other people's chests like this."

His chuckle was deep, vibrating through his body. She drew in another breath, thinking he really did smell good.

"I usually don't find myself in a closet with women I've just met, but this isn't so bad."

His words made her laugh, releasing some of the stress. The wind died down, and it didn't seem so bad. She tried to take a step back, but they had no room in this small space.

He sighed before he moved his hand from her back and opened the door. She wished his hand was back on her, but now there wasn't any reason for him to touch her. She stepped out into the hall, fear twisting through her at what she would find. Noah was right beside her, his eyebrows raised.

"Do you think there was any damage?" he asked.

"I don't—" she took a step toward the reception desk but paused as the wind picked up. She could hear the wind noise, which wasn't good.

"I don't think this is safe," Noah said as he took her hand, pulling her next to him.

She glanced up, staring into his eyes. No question, he really was very good looking. Noah kept his gaze on her as he drew in a slow breath. The way he was looking at her and the slight curve of his lips was sensual, or she thought it was. She was probably overblowing his reaction. Then he took a step closer. Her heart sped up. His hand came up and cupped her cheek, his thumb smoothing over her skin. Her breath caught in her throat and her knees went weak.

Keeley could count the number of times on one hand a good-looking guy had paid attention to her. If Noah kissed her, she would put everything she had into it, because things like this just never happened to women like her.

He opened his mouth and was about to say something when she heard the door open and someone step in.

"Keeley, are you in here?" Doc Julian called out from the front. Perfectly bad timing.

"Yes," she said loud enough for him to hear her as she stepped away from Noah. Disappointment filled her. This man was the first good-looking guy to take an interest in her in eons.

Noah flashed an apologetic smile before he stepped away and moved closer to the sound of Doc Julian's voice.

"Hello, I'm your eight o'clock. I showed up early, and we hid in the closet during the storm."

"Oh, hey. Gosh, I'm sorry, I don't think I'll be able to do anything today. Are you hurting?"

"No, sir. I just needed to have you check on something since I just moved here. My previous dentist wanted me to see someone for an old filling. It can wait."

Keeley took a step into the exam room at the end, shock filling her. The window had shattered, and in its place was a gaping hole. Glass and tree debris had scattered over the room and water puddled on the floor. They wouldn't be working today. They'd have to find someone to help clean the mess up.

"Keeley." Doc Julian put his hands on her shoulder and turned her around. "Your car, it has a tree on it."

"What? My car?" Her gaze roved over the glass on the floor then back to Doc before she glanced at Noah. She should be moving, but her mind was racing from the window to Noah and then her car. It was too much.

She took a step toward the front of the building then hesitated.

"Go look," Doc Julian said. "We'll start cleaning up in a bit. You need to see your car."

She took a few more steps then sped up, almost running by the time she was in the front reception room. There were cars in the lot now, but only four. Her stomach dropped. Of course, it was just her luck. Her car was the only one with a tree flattening the roof, front windshield destroyed, hood crinkled around the root ball of the tree.

"I'm glad you weren't in it," Doc Julian said beside her.

Tears sprang to her eyes, but she swiped them away.

Crying wouldn't help. When would life get better? She couldn't take another terrible thing happening. Now she had no vehicle and no way to get a new one. She didn't make enough to really save, not for a car, and she had nothing to fall back on. Life couldn't get any worse, could it?

CHAPTER TWO

A TORNADO, THAT WAS A FIRST. NOAH HAD BEEN through a lot, maybe more than most who never saw military action. Those guys were hardcore. His FBI experience was varied since he was a member of the Special Tactics and Weapons Team. In some areas, the FBI SWAT team didn't get much action. In Miami, he'd seen a lot, and he'd heard the same about San Antonio.

Moving to Texas was just supposed to be a step up on his career path, but if he met someone, someone like Keeley, he may not ever want to leave. She was beautiful, sexy, funny, and she'd felt awesome up against his body.

It had taken concentration not to get hard. Keeley's hands had made him want to investigate her mouth and more. He shouldn't think that way about her. She would probably be pissed if she knew he'd wanted to push her up against the wall and kiss her until they both forgot their names.

Next week, when he showed back up for his appointment, he'd have to ask her out. He should have before he left the dentist's office today, but she'd been busy with her car and working to clean the office. He prayed she was single. No way would he involve himself with a married woman, even one as hot as Keeley. That kind of shit was stupid. He'd had friends on both sides of that equation, and all he ever saw was hurt.

His phone buzzed, and he answered on the second ring. "Special Agent Noah Grey, how can I help you."

"Agent Grey, it's Harry Simmons, I'm in town at the field office this morning, wondering how you were doing."

Harry's chuckle warmed him. He'd known Harry for years, and for some reason, the older FBI agent had decided to mentor him.

"Great. Just headed that way."

"You're running late this morning. I was wondering if you blew away with that tornado?"

He chuckled. "Actually, I was right where it hit. I had a dentist appointment, and the office lost a window, probably some other damage, but everyone is okay."

"Jesus, son," Simmons's voice changed, became more serious. "Here I was pulling your leg. Are you okay?"

"Yes, sir. I'm about a minute away from the office. I'll fill you in after I get a cup of coffee."

"Sure thing, and I'm sorry you had to live through a tornado in one of your first few weeks here."

"It's okay, sir. I'm happy to be here, even with the tornados and all."

Simmons ended the call right when the office came into view. He was happy to see Harry. He'd been here almost two months and didn't know too many people. The job was the job, not much different than Miami, but it was the people who made one office better than another. So far, he'd been too busy to do much more than meet the people in his unit.

South Texas was having issues with people crossing the border, not coming here, but being taken away against their will. In addition to acting as a gateway for human traffickers, drugs were streaming in like hotcakes. Mainly because Texas had three hundred and sixty-seven miles of coasts where day-trippers could end up being mules for the drug cartels. They'd go out fishing and hook-up with some drug runner instead of catching fish. The runners would send them back to shore with a little more than a grouper or sea bass packed in ice. It was too hard to monitor every single inch of the coastline, and though the Coast Guard was trying to make a dent, they couldn't stop every fishing boat on the water. The FBI had stationed him in San Antonio instead of Houston or another town close to the coast because they didn't want him to have to evacuate if a hurricane hit.

He'd helped Florida get a handle on coordinating agencies, but Texas was a tough nut to crack. Every single little police station and sheriff's office wanted to handle the problem their own way. They didn't want to tell any other agencies, even agencies based in Texas, what was going on. Add to the mess, the bigger agencies inside of Texas weren't sharing information with each other. If this issue were small, it wouldn't matter, but millions of pounds of cocaine streamed into the country by boat each year. With twenty-five interstate highways and over two hundred sixty-eight thousand square miles of space, it was a drug runners' paradise when you added in agencies that didn't want to communicate.

He pulled into the parking lot of the FBI office and cut the engine. This area wasn't any worse for wear. Actually, it looked the same, just wet. He should have grabbed Keeley's number. He wanted to text her and ask if she was really okay. Next week, he'd get her number no matter what.

Inside, people were gathered in small groups, chatting about the storm. He picked up bits of conversation as he moved past eight different groups of people discussing how they'd been affected by the morning storm. It had knocked out power around the city, roads had been shut down, schools had gone into special storm mode, and daycares were calling parents informing them their kids were safe.

He sighed and took the stairs up to the second floor. He'd given up family for the FBI. That wasn't really a fair assessment of what had happened. Young love had caught him, but Traci hadn't been willing to give even an inch. In the end, he'd been too tired to stay with her. She'd wanted him to change everything, and he couldn't give up his dreams. He'd grown up poor, and his mom had died of a meth overdose when he'd turned seventeen. It had shaped who he was and what he wanted to do in life.

Being an agent had been everything. He'd worked two jobs to earn enough to attend a local community college, then he'd transferred those credits to a state school. After earning his undergraduate degree, he'd spent two years waiting tables, seeing how cocaine ruined chefs and wait-ers, ripping their families apart, even killing some of them before he'd applied to Columbia University and been accepted with a partial scholarship. He'd received grants too and graduated with only ten thousand in student loans. The day he'd been accepted into Quantico, it had been the best day of his life.

Now that he was established in his career and had a reasonably good handle on his professional life, he was ready for a personal one. It wasn't so easy, though. Hookup applications weren't his style. He realized early on he wasn't going to meet someone who wanted long-term on those things. He'd tried the general dating apps, and it seemed like he didn't meet people he actually wanted to spend time with. At clubs and bars, it was the same. He really wanted to meet a nice person who just enjoyed hanging out, watching movies, maybe reading, and wouldn't freak out if he had to overnight in Houston, Padre, Port Lavaca, or any number of small Texas towns because they had information about a drug shipment coming in.

Maybe he was past his prime. He'd turned thirty-two last month, and though he still hit the gym regularly, the gains and losses were harder to achieve. Pizza tended to stick on his belly and muscles were more challenging to build if he didn't stick with it.

"There he is," Harry Simmons called out. "It's good to see you."

Harry worked out of the DC office for years and spent every Tuesday at Quantico, teaching the new recruits. They'd developed a bond when Harry learned that he'd grown up one block over from where Harry had, of course, Harry was fifteen years older so they never would have met.

"How are you doing?" Noah stepped up and hugged Harry. Normally he wouldn't hug anyone he worked with, much less someone like Harry Simmons who'd attained Executive Assistant Director status, but they were friends. The man had worked hard and somehow achieved a balance in life and was still married to the same woman, and his kids liked him. His daughter, Selma, was at Quantico now, going through the program to become an agent.

"It's good to see you. So tell me, how is San Antonio treating you?"

"It's good. I like it better than Miami."

Harry's eyebrows lifted. "Really?"

His lips curved up in a smile. Harry had always pressed him on everything, even his personal life. "I know, Miami has all those women on the beach, and it was fun for the first few months, but I've changed."

"Want some stability?" Harry laughed. "Maybe you'll find someone here."

His mind flashed to Keeley and his body warmed. "I think stability sounds nice."

"Well, good, you're in the right place. Special Agent in Charge, Michael Spears, is a good man. Have you met him yet?"

"No sir, I haven't had the pleasure. I believe he was out of town when I showed up."

"Come with me." Harry stepped into a conference room and waved me in.

He followed, thinking about everything waiting on him at his desk. He needed to get on the ball and get some meetings arranged.

Simmons strolled up to a man dressed in a dark suit, wire glasses, who looked to be in his fifties and very serious. "Michael, this is Noah Grey. I've known him for years. One of my favorite students at the Academy."

Spears lifted his eyebrows and then cut his gaze to Noah. "I didn't think you picked favorites."

Harry chuckled and shook his head. "You caught me. I do and I've only ever had one favorite. He's a good man too."

"Hello, sir. It's nice to meet you." He shook Spears's hand. The man was younger than Harry but didn't seem to smile as much. He appeared to be sharp like he took in information quickly and assessed the situation with lightning speed. After a second, the man cracked a smile. Noah breathed a sigh of relief.

"It's good to meet you too. Executive Assistant Director Simmons told me you experienced a tornado this morning."

"Call me Simmons," Harry said.

Spears' lips quirked up, and he nodded before speaking again. "The tornado, was it bad?"

Noah's lips thinned. How should he answer? "It knocked out one window. But we survived. Everyone is okay, except for one car in the lot that was smashed by a tree."

"Oh, that's bad. It took me a few years to get used to them. My wife hates the storms, but we're happy here. She enjoys the warm winters. Says she never wants to move back to the freezing cold she grew up with in Wisconsin."

"I've never been there, but I hear those are brutal."

"They are," Spears said as he took a seat. "Join us for a moment before our meeting starts. I see on your file that you're also testing for our SWAT team. We could use another guy with your skillset."

"Thank you, sir," Noah said. "It's a responsibility I'm honored to take."

"I'm glad you think that way. We're in a difficult area. The crime rate is growing, drugs are more prevalent, human trafficking is huge here. It seems like as soon as we get a handle on one thing, something else worse comes up."

He nodded, "I hope I can make a dent here in Texas like I did in Florida."

"We do too," Spears said.

"The first few weeks has been spent clearing work left waiting. I've set up a few appointments with various agencies throughout the state and will make more today. It's slow going, but I need a foundation to work with, one that will hopefully stop the flow of drugs into Texas. Inter-organizational cooperation, especially with the small departments along the coast, is my goal for this half of the year."

Spears barked out a harsh laugh. "If you can get that down here, I'll be impressed."

They chatted for a few more minutes before their meeting started. Noah headed to his own office, making sure to send a note to Simmons, thanking him for the introduction to Spears. The man had helped him so many times in his career and he had no real idea why.

After the slow start to his day, he finished up late, and headed home, assessing the damage the town had suffered. The apartment he'd rented had escaped the tornado, but one down the street had been hit. Eventually, he'd buy a house if he stayed in this area, for now, he was happy to rent.

He flicked on the news as he heated a microwave dinner and opened a beer. His chest felt tight and he rubbed at it as worry for Keeley blossomed. He should have kissed her. She'd felt just right in his arms. Why hadn't he gotten her number? Was she okay after the storms? He had to push away his worry for her, or he'd go crazy trying to find out information about her. The last thing he needed to do was use his resources to look her up. Next week would be soon enough.

CHAPTER THREE

KEELEY WAS GLAD DOC JULIAN HAD WANTED TO GET the office open as soon as possible. They'd worked all day cleaning the mess the storm had left. Her car had been totaled. It still sat in the lot because the towing companies had been busy and couldn't pick it up until today. Luckily she didn't owe any money on the car but having a car payment was the last thing she needed.

They finished with their first patient and moved to the cubbies where she kept her purse. Sharron, the receptionist, had just answered a call

"Yes, sir. Of course," Sharron said. "Who?"

She shouldn't be eavesdropping, but it was hard not to in this small front area.

"Keeley Anderson? Yes, she's fine. Okay, we'll see you next week."

Keeley stepped around the corner and lifted her brows. "What was that about?" she asked.

Sharron's lips turned up in a secretive smile. "That patient who was here yesterday morning during the tornado. He was asking to make sure everything was okay."

"Oh." Her stomach twisted as memories of him holding her surfaced. The guy had been hot, and she'd been desperate. He was probably just asking to be nice. She shouldn't think anything of him asking about her at all.

Work sucked her back in, and at four, Doc Julian had some guys come by to give an estimate on the window. There was something off about the workers, but Doc Julian wouldn't listen to her. It was his money, and she had no real say in what happened to the office, so she kept quiet. The work would be done in the evening on Thursday, and then they would be gone. She was glad the crew could get to it fast because for now, they had only one room available, which meant they couldn't get to as many patients, which seemed to irritate Doc.

On Friday morning, she was again the first to arrive because of a storm, and she'd had to leave her apartment early since she didn't have a car. Luckily she lived close by, and the walk was quick. The window had been fixed, and it looked good. She shouldn't have been worried about the guys Doc Julian had hired.

She put her bag in her cubby and made sure the bathroom had plenty of floss, mouthwash, cups for the mouthwash, toothpaste, and toothbrushes. The last thing they wanted was to work on someone's mouth who needed to brush but didn't have the supplies available. Usually, they only went through five toothbrushes a day, which wasn't too bad.

She entered the small kitchenette area and made sure there wasn't anything too gross in the refrigerator before checking under the sink. When she opened the cabinet door, she paused.

"What is this?"

She grabbed the bag she didn't recognize and put it on

the countertop. It looked like packages of medicine no one had opened. She sighed and set them on the table before turning to grab the scissors. Sometimes medicine came wrapped up with cooling packs. If this were something that had to be refrigerated, it would probably be ruined. The last thing she wanted was to be held responsible for someone else messing up. Maybe, just maybe the cooling packs would still be cold, and the medicine wouldn't be ruined.

She cut into the first pack, anger driving her moves. The blade of the scissors slid in and white powder puffed out. She stopped, fearing she'd done something wrong.

The front door opened, and Sharron called out. "Anyone here."

"I'm in the kitchen," she hollered back, wishing she hadn't just made such a huge mess.

Sharron came around the corner and down the hall, talking about the party for her three-year-old child she was planning for Sunday afternoon.

"But I don't want to have a bunch of balloons. I don't think people realize there is a real shortage of helium. I mean, sure balloons are pretty, but the—what is that?"

Sharron's eyes were wide, and her mouth open. She narrowed her gaze and stepped closer.

"Oh God," Sharron said. "I know what that is."

"What is it? I found the package under the sink, and I thought it was medicine, but it's powder. Did I screw something up?" Panic filled her as worry over her actions inflated.

"You have no idea what you just did?" Sharron lifted her brows.

The panic inside amplified. "No," Keeley whined.

The front door opened, and her fear increased.

Someone else had arrived before she could hide her mistake.

"Oh God, I'm going to be in trouble, aren't I?" Her voice was thin and high pitched as her chest tightened.

Sharron cocked one eyebrow. "Someone is going to be in trouble, but I don't think it's you."

She stared at the powder on her hands, wondering if she could just tape the package up and pretend this hadn't happened. "Who then?"

"Hello ladies," Doc Julian said as he came around the corner. "I'm glad to see—what's that?"

"I found the bag under the sink," Keeley said. "I thought it was medicines. You know sometimes they come wrapped in plastic, and I thought I'd missed this one. I don't know what it is."

"I know what it is." Doc Julian bit his lip, and his eyes narrowed. "Shit, this is bad."

He sounded worried, and the wrinkles around his eyes increased as his lips thinned out. Now Keeley was doing more than panicking. She hadn't meant to do anything wrong. She lifted her hand and chewed her nail, surprised at the bitter flavor. Then her mouth went numb. All of her mouth, even her tongue. She pulled her hand away from her face, staring at her fingers.

"We don't need this." Julian turned and took a few steps, then turned back. "Oh God, I have to call the cops. I don't know who brought this in. Keeley, do you swear you didn't—"

She threw up her hands, noticing the fine powder floating in the air around her. "I don't even know what it is. I found it this morning in the cabinet under the sink. You know how I go through and make sure stuff is clean when I get here? I replaced the toothbrushes, checked the supplies, then came in here. I was about to make coffee after I checked the refrigerator. I looked under the sink to check for food and other things like trash and found this. I really thought it was our medicine. Am I in trouble?"

Doc shook his head. "No. No, you didn't do anything wrong."

"What is going on then? My tongue is numb. What is this stuff?" she wailed as tears threatened.

"It's cocaine."

Doc's words made her heart speed up. She dropped the knife and stepped back, seeing the white powder on her scrubs and her fingers. "Oh shit, I have cocaine on me. What do I do?"

"Nothing," Doc said. "Just calm down, and I'll call the cops."

"Are you sure?" Sharron asked.

"I can't have this in my office," Doc said. "If it's yours tell me now because the cops are going to find out."

"Hold on," Sharron said as she lifted her hands. "It has been years since I did any street drugs. I wasn't an angel when I was younger, but I didn't deal drugs, and I don't do that now."

"Okay, I didn't think it was yours," Doc said.

"Whose could it be?" Sharron asked.

"No clue." Doc grabbed his chin and pulled. His gaze stayed on the table where the cocaine sat. "I don't think anyone who works here would deal."

"Those guys," Keeley said.

Doc glanced up. "Which ones?"

"I felt odd when the people fixing the window were here. I don't know, just an odd feeling. I don't like to think they are the people responsible, but why else would a huge bag of cocaine be at the office?"

"This sucks," Sharron said.

"It really does," Doc added.

She glanced down at her hands, wondering if this cocaine would have any long-term effects. She didn't like drugs and hadn't ever taken them. But she guessed she had now. Oh God, she'd taken drugs. Panic rose as she thought about it.

After Doc called a friend on the force, he came over and put his arm around her.

"You feeling okay?"

She glanced up and nodded. "Yeah. Actually I feel very good."

"You should clean up your hands."

She glanced down and stared at them. "Yeah." He was right. She couldn't be walking around with cocaine all over her.

She moved to the bathroom and washed her hands then wiped away the powder on the front of her shirt and pants. The first patient showed up, signaling a start to their day.

After they finished with the first two patients, the cops arrived. They wanted to know exactly what happened. She cried as she explained how the powder had been all over her hands and shirt. At first, she thought they wouldn't believe her, but she guessed she'd said the right things. They wanted to run her fingerprints just to make sure they knew her prints and could eliminate them from the search when they dusted the packages.

It only took an hour for them to process the cocaine. Keeley had expected the cops to take her in even though she was innocent. It seemed like these days people didn't believe others no matter what.

The cops left without her, which surprised the heck out of her. All weekend long she worried about the cocaine. Even when she showed up at the police station and had her fingerprints taken, she still felt like she should have known.

On Monday, she arrived late because the weather had turned and she had to go back to her apartment and get an umbrella. "Sorry, I'm late. The rain got me. At least I didn't have to deal with any cocaine."

"Cocaine?" The voice was low and not at all who she was expecting.

The sexy guy from last week, the one who'd shared the closet with her during the tornado, was here.

"You're early," Keeley said.

He stood and moved to her. "I am. Doc Julian called me last night and asked me to show up early. He's in there now getting everything ready."

"Oh crud." She rushed back to the patient rooms and almost ran into Doc. "I'm so sorry. I didn't know he was coming in early."

"No worries. Really, it's okay. I didn't want to bother you since I know you don't have a car yet and it was raining hard. Glad you made it." Doc shot her a huge grin, softening his words.

"Ugh, I need to do something about a car. But they are expensive. I'm not sure what I'll end up doing. I'm sorry I'm late."

"Don't worry, it's fine."

She felt off like she hadn't had any coffee this morning. "I'll wash up and get everything else ready, and then you can start working."

"Sure, and Keeley, really, don't worry."

She put away her things into the cubby and used the restroom before washing her hands. Her stomach twisted when she'd seen the guy and desire had filled her. She was being stupid. There wasn't any way a guy like him would want her. There wasn't anything special about her.

Once Doc Julian had everything he needed, she called Noah back and asked him to take a seat.

"Do you need anything before we start?"

His quick smile made her warm. "No, I'm good." He met her gaze, and his eyes looked so serious. "So what cocaine?"

Doc Julian walked in right then and grunted. "We found some cocaine hidden in our office. Actually, Keeley did. She had no clue what it was, and by the time I showed up she'd cut into the brick, and it was all over her."

"Really?" Noah asked as he turned to stare at her.

"Yes, really." She handed Doc Julian his gloves as they took a seat. "I've never done drugs. I mean, I drank in high school, but I didn't do things like cocaine or even weed, still haven't. Well, I guess I did with the cocaine because it did puff out and get into my nose and it was on my fingers, and some got in my mouth, but I didn't feel too weird, and by the time I started work I was fine."

"Do they know whose it was?" Noah asked.

"No clue," Doc said before he placed his hand on Noah's shoulder. "I'm going to lean you back and take a look."

"Sure."

Doc Julian continued to talk while he looked at the filling in Noah's tooth. It took only a moment before he sat up and pushed the button so Julian could sit up too.

"Okay, so here's the deal. You need that replaced. It's pulled back in a few places. I would suggest you do it sooner rather than later. I have enough time to take care of it right now, and then you won't have to come back again, that's why I asked you to show up early."

He grimaced. He hated dental work but knew it had to get done. "Sure, let's do it."

"Good." Doc Julian smiled. "Keeley, would you set me up for ceramic."

"Yes, sir."

"Okay, Noah, we're going to lay you back down and take care of this fast. Don't worry, it will all be over with soon."

Doc was a master with shots and was up and out of his chair before she returned with the tools they would need.

Noah kind of sat up and looked at her when she walked back in. "Hey, how is your car?"

She huffed out a breath. "It's dead."

"Are you going to get a new one?"

"No, probably not. It's so expensive." She tried to sound like it was no big deal to not have a car though it really was. "I don't want to have to deal with a payment right now."

"Oh, so how are you getting around."

She shrugged. "I'm walking."

"Um..."

He trailed off, and she turned to look at him. "Yes."

"Would you go out with me — like dinner, um, tonight? I don't know the area, and I thought it would be nice to, well, you know have someone outside of work to talk to."

His question shocked her, and she stood with her mouth open long enough for Doc to come back in. His lips were quirked up in a smile; he'd obviously overheard.

"You should go," Doc said.

"I-I, Doc Julian, I don't know that it's appropriate."

"It's okay," Doc said. "You're not his doctor, and he's not yours. I think you should give him a chance. He's nice, an FBI agent, and he's not too bad looking."

Heat filled her face. "Doc, can you just fill his tooth and let me figure out how to say yes."

Noah chuckled and seemed to relax as the doctor went to work. Doc finished quickly, and Noah was sitting up the next time she stepped into the room.

"So is that a yes?" Noah asked.

She groaned and heat filled her face. "That was so awkward. Are you sure you want to go out with me?"

He nodded. "I am."

"Even though I'm awkward, and everything around me gets awkward?"

That made him chuckle. "Yes, and I don't think you're awkward."

Her face heated even more. Noah was too good looking for her, but she liked him. It would be nice to go out on a date with a guy she found interesting. His job concerned her, mainly because she didn't know how she would deal with him being in danger.

"Okay, so I guess we're going out. I don't have a car, but I can Uber anywhere."

"I can pick you up," Noah said then shot her a lopsided frown because his mouth wouldn't obey. "Or is that too much? I don't want you feeling nervous."

"It's okay. You're an FBI agent, right? And you asked me out in front of my boss, so he knows who I'm with and if I end up missing, they'll know who did it."

He chuckled. "It would look bad on my FBI dossier if you disappeared."

Her mouth dropped open. "So that's the only think keeping you from doing something wrong?"

He bit his lower lip and she wanted to taste that lip too. The man was the sexiest guy she'd ever met.

"Not the only thing, though I would like to have you to

myself for a few hours." His voice had gone all low and sexy, making her warm.

She lifted her brows and he gave a half-smile. Doc Julian stepped in and sat on his stool.

"I'm going to lean you back and take a look at my work."

Two minutes later, Noah was up and ready to go. "What is your phone number and I'll text you when I'm done with work. I say aim for six this evening, but I am expected to drop everything if we get a huge break in a case."

"Sure, let me give you my number." She wrote it down and handed it to him. He pulled out his phone and entered it immediately.

"I don't want to lose this. I'll call you around six, and I'll get your address then."

She nodded, feeling a little weird about him having her number. Usually, she didn't hand out her number. She'd rather have a less traceable, easier to block method of communication, but she trusted Noah.

After he left, she floated on cloud nine. It was odd being asked this morning to go out, but she was happy she didn't have to wait a week or so before she saw him again. She couldn't believe a guy like Noah wanted to date plain-old her. She wasn't anything special, not really.

CHAPTER FOUR

NOAH HADN'T MEANT TO ASK HER OUT, HE'D WANTED her number, but being there, seeing her face again, he couldn't let her get away. When she hadn't answered, he'd freaked out, thinking she didn't want to go out with him. That had been awkward. All of it made him feel like he was back in high school asking someone on a date who was so far out of his league they didn't exist in the same universe.

When she'd made a comment about the cocaine, he'd been freaked out at first. The explanation of what happened was so comical he couldn't help but want to spend time with her. The cocaine worried him, though. If she were working with someone who was dealing, that wouldn't be good. He would look into it and find out any information he could.

When he hit the office, he was pulled into an emergency meeting. The San Antonio police had served a warrant for drug possession, and a cop had been shot. The guys in the house fled and picked up a four-year-old girl who'd been riding her bike down the sidewalk. They were holding her as a bargaining chip. Somehow, the police lost track of the car, and they didn't know where the drug runners had taken the girl. The FBI was brought in to help find the girl and bring the assholes to justice who had kidnapped a helpless child.

Noah began tracking down all of the information on the guys in the house. He looked for known associates, family, any connection that could lead them to the little girl. For two hours, it was all hands on deck. Then one small piece of information turned into two and then three, and suddenly they had a snowball rolling down the hill, aiming right at the men who had kidnapped the kid.

San Antonio police agreed that the FBI SWAT team should go in. In Miami, Noah would have been first up, but here, he hadn't been assigned to the team yet. He watched from the sidelines, wishing he could go in and deliver pain to these assholes. Of course, he would do it by the book, but jerks like these guys always fired or tried to fight back. Many of them would end up dead before the day was over because the FBI didn't play when going in for a raid.

A guy stepped up beside him, watching the closed-circuit video of the SWAT team headed in. "You wish you were out there, right? Cody Whittaker, by the way."

"I sure do. Noah Grey, it's nice to meet you." They shook hands and then turned back to watching the screen.

"The team is good. Only the best. I heard you were trying for it," Cody said.

Noah nodded. "I've been a member of the SWAT team since my first assignment."

"Good for you. I wouldn't mind going to the range with you. I'm sure you have pointers that could help me."

Noah glanced to Cody and nodded. "Sure."

He turned back to the screen and watched as SWAT breached the door. Breaching was the job he usually got.

The guy doing this job seemed flawless. There was competition for spots on the teams here, and he would have to work hard to make it. He had confidence in his abilities, but so did the rest of the guys. Luckily for him, there were multiple SWAT teams and back up members so he'd at least make one of the backup groups if he didn't place on one of the main units.

Once the door was open, he held his breath for a second, praying no one got shot. The FBI used every technology available, so they knew where the men were, but there could always be surprises when entering an unknown house or building.

Shots were fired and returned quickly. Noah kept up with the body count. Eight of the drug runners were down, some still breathing, but most had put the SWAT team into the position where they had to take a kill shot.

After fifteen minutes, the team called the all-clear. Noah blew out a breath, and Cody patted him on the back.

"None of ours were hit," Cody said. "So what made you come down to the scene?"

Noah met his gaze. "I'm heading up the initiative to reduce drugs coming in at the coast."

Cody nodded. "I'm in the organized crime unit."

"We should talk," Noah said. "Let me get your phone number, and I'll text later."

"I have an hour free after this, want to get lunch," Cody asked. "I'm guessing that you, like most of the rest of us, haven't eaten."

Noah chuckled. "Nope, I haven't. I'll be sifting paper from this mess for months. Let's walk through, then head out to grab something, and we can discuss how to work together."

"Thank you, sir."

"Sir?" Noah lifted his eyebrows and shot Cody a look.

"Well, it's obvious you're older than me and more senior."

Noah smiled and nodded. "You're funny."

Cody returned his smile. "Thanks."

Noah spent forty minutes in the building, making sure everything he would need was taken to the warehouse where it would be processed before being cataloged. He felt confident they would have all the information. He caught up to Cody, and they drove about a mile to a small restaurant that was filled with other agents with their heads bent over food, talking in low tones.

He and Cody grabbed a menu and took a seat. In minutes, they placed their order and were talking about how they could coordinate.

"Both of us are working on similar problems," Cody said.

"We are." Noah took a sip of tea. "I feel like we're on a beach with a rising tide racing toward us. I don't know if it's going to overwhelm us or if it will slow and we'll stay ahead of it."

"I don't like the idea of it getting worse." Cody placed his phone on the table, screen down. He shook his head then leaned in like the rest of the agents were, speaking low so no one else could pick up what they were saying. "I've heard that a new gang is expanding. Lots of cocaine. They're mean too. They've gone beyond using their usual mules, now they're using working people."

"Really?" Noah flashed back to what Keeley had said about the cocaine. Could the bricks she'd found be someone in her office? He had a bad feeling. Tonight, they would talk about that. He didn't want their date to be only about serious stuff though.

"That look on your face, what was it about?"

He shook his head, then glanced around. "I was at the dentist earlier. Someone who works there found some cocaine in the office. The local PD is handling it, but I think I need to get involved."

"You think there's more to it? Like the dentist is in on it? That would be something new. We thought it wasn't professionals, just construction and restaurant workers."

"I'm not sure," Noah said. "It sounded like everyone at the office was in the clear, but it had to be someone."

"Once you figure out what happened, come talk to me. Think I need to know."

"Sure deal."

Their food arrived. Noah had ordered enchiladas since they were soft. The filling didn't really hurt, but he didn't want to test it by eating something too hard.

They talked about San Antonio and a few things about the office. Noah asked about entertainment in the area, and Cody told him about some activities, mentioning an entertainment complex with laser tag, mini-golf, and go-carts.

After their meal, Cody dropped him at the scene, and he went back in, talking to a few of the people who were still there. They would have their work cut out for them if they wanted to stop this kind of thing from happening again.

At least the little girl would go home alive. He hoped the parents got her counseling because she sure as heck would need it.

It was a little after six when he stepped out of the office and texted Keeley. She replied almost automatically with her address. He opened his trunk and pulled out a short sleeve collared shirt, deciding it would do. He learned early in his career to have a fresh set of clothes, both casual and work, in the trunk of his car. He cycled them out every Sunday and put in fresh clothes. He also kept a change of shoes and socks at the ready.

The shirt he'd pulled on wasn't his favorite, but at least it wasn't FBI logoed. He kept two of those in a drawer in his office. Being an agent meant always being prepared even for the unexpected like having a casual shirt at the ready.

Anticipation filled him on the fifteen-minute drive to her apartment. The place wasn't far from the FBI head-quarters. He took in the area and figured out she didn't live in a great neighborhood. The place was old, which didn't bother him, but the gang activity did.

His worry increased when a guy stepped out of the apartment right next to Keeley's and stared him down. He said hello, but the nicety wasn't returned.

Keeley pulled open her door and stepped out, a huge smile on her face. "You ready?" She looked to her left and smiled. "Hello, Mr. Brice. I hope you all are having a good week."

Brice grunted then turned and went back into his apartment.

"What's up with him?" Noah asked.

Keeley waved her hand in the air and shook her head. "He's just intense. He doesn't like people." Keeley turned and locked her door, giving it a shove before stepping away.

A slimy feeling snaked up his back, and he glanced around, looking for someone watching them. He didn't see anything on his way to his car, but the weird feeling didn't leave him.

He opened the passenger door for Keeley before going around to his side of the car. The engine purred when he turned the key. He'd bought a mustang for personal use four years ago and loved driving it.

"I have the perfect place. It's not too far."

"Good. So how is your tooth?"

Keeley's question made him smile. It was weird dating someone. They'd spent time together in that little closet, so he felt like he knew her a little bit, but this was different. An awkwardness slid through him. He didn't want to screw this up, which of course meant he'd probably screw something up.

The light ahead went to red, so he slowed and turned to look at her. He couldn't believe she was in his car. She was looking at him now, and time seemed to stop. Something inside clicked, like this was one of those moments he wanted to remember forever. She was beautiful, smart, sweet, and he needed her.

"You look nice." His voice seemed weird, kind of far off, like he was somehow detached from his body, floating above this all, observing. He wished he could stay with her always.

Her lips tilted up. "Thank you. So do you."

The car behind him honked and he jumped. They both chuckled as he eased off the brake and put his foot on the accelerator. "I didn't have time to shower. I wish I had, but it would have been seven or later by the time I got over here."

He turned into a parking lot, excited to take her to a pub he'd found that served a variety of food. What he'd eaten so far at the place was excellent. But in the parking lot were two buses full of kids who were spilling out and blocking the entrance to the building.

"Oh no," Amber said. "That won't be relaxing at all."

"Yikes. I mean, I don't mind kids, but I don't want to spend the evening screaming over them." He turned around in the lot and headed out. "Now I don't know where to go."

"I know a good place," Keeley said.

"Sure, just tell me how to get there."

"Turn right here and make a right at the light," she said.

He'd wanted to plan an awesome night with Keeley, but maybe this would be great too. She could relax somewhere she was comfortable. He made the turns and drove about two minutes when Keeley pointed to the left.

"The yellow sign about a half-mile up. Turn in there and then go to the back of the lot."

He glanced around, thinking the area looked sketchy. Maybe Keeley was used to living here. In Miami, he'd gotten used to the areas some might think were terrible. Though he was still in the same country, each region was different. The social norms in one city would be considered unacceptable in another area. When he'd lived in Virginia, it had been a culture shock because of how pristine the place was. In San Antonio, the people were different, the customs strange to him. He liked the area, but like Miami, it would take some getting used to.

He drove into the lot, and behind the first building, he found a brightly lit restaurant with music spilling out. He parked and turned to Keeley, smiling to indicate his appreciation.

"How did you find this place?"

She shrugged like it was no big deal. "I've lived in the area for a long time. Also, it's cheap."

"Cheap, like do I need to worry about the food cheap?" Noah asked.

She chuckled and shook her head as she opened the door. He jumped out and rushed around, but she already had the door closed and was standing beside the car.

"I wish you would have let me do that."

She stood with her hips cocked to one side. "I can open my own car door."

"I'm sure you can, but when I take you out, I want to do nice things for you like open your door."

Her lips thinned, and she shook her head. "It really doesn't make sense to me."

He held up one hand. "Okay, so how about I tell you when I want to open the door."

She narrowed her gaze at him and shrugged. "Does it really mean that much to you?"

"Yes, for some crazy reason, it does."

"Okay, if you'll promise me that if I pick out a movie, you'll watch it with me even if it's not your favorite."

Panic raced in. He was a movie snob, well maybe not a snob, but he liked certain types of movies. "Wait, but what if it's not good?"

She chuckled and took his arm, patting his bicep with her other hand. "A deal's a deal."

"I think you got the better end of this deal."

"I don't know, you don't know my taste in movies."

They were close to the door, and he stepped fast to pull it open. She walked by, and the air drifted out. The scent of amazing Mexican food hit. He moaned.

"Señorita Keeley, and you brought a friend."

"This is Noah." Keeley's lips spread into a sweet smile. Her cheeks turned pink when she looked at him. "Noah, Señor Gonzalo. He and his wife run this place."

Noah shook the man's hand. "It's nice to meet you."

Señor Gonzalo gave him a broad smile. "Thank you. We'll give you a table near the fountain. It's quieter back there, and other people can't hear you talk."

Señor Gonzalo led them past the tables at the front to a section behind a tan stucco wall with black ironwork in the open spaces. A fountain bubbled in the center of the room, drowning out the sounds of the kitchen and the front dining area, offering some privacy.

It seemed like Señor Gonzalo liked romance. He appreciated what the man was doing for them. He liked the restaurant and he felt like maybe this was a better choice. He hoped Keeley and he meshed well. He wanted to see her more than just once, and it wasn't just her looks, he liked her.

Chips and salsa were brought over along with water. He took a quick glance at the menu and ordered grilled chicken with peppers.

"I hope you don't mind Mexican food," Keeley said.

"No, it's great. I lived in Miami before this and ate Cuban food all the time. It's different, but I like it. Mexican food isn't too far of a leap from Cuban. I also enjoy Italian and some French cuisine."

Keeley picked up a chip and dipped it into the salsa. "So now you're here. And do you like San Antonio?"

"I do." He picked up a chip, dipped it in the salsa then took a bite. The salsa was hot with peppers and had a hearty, meaty flavor.

"That's good," he said as he pulled out another chip.

"It is. How long do you think you'll stay here?"

He shrugged as he grabbed another chip. "I don't know. This was a fairly big promotion, and there's a lot of work to be done. I think I'll be here for a few years."

Keeley leaned in and her eyebrows raised. "Can you tell me what you do?"

His lips quirked up. "Basically, I try to stop drugs from entering the country."

Keeley's hands stopped halfway to her mouth, the chip dripping salsa onto the vinyl tablecloth.

"Like the stuff I found in the office? That was weird." Keeley bit into her chip and then set the leftover part onto the small plate beside her. "I've never seen drugs. I had no clue they even shipped them that way. Seriously, I think I breathed some of the dust in because I didn't even know what it was. It was all over my shirt and pants like I'd been baking cookies with loads of flour and couldn't contain my excitement while stirring."

The way she described it made him laugh. "I'm glad nothing bad happened. I need to call the local police and see what I can find out."

She blinked at him. "Why?"

"Well, for one, it's my job, and two, you don't know who brought the drugs into the office. Really, it could be bad."

She shrugged. "I know everyone who works there. There is no way one of them did something awful like bring in drugs."

He ate another chip before he spoke. "It's weird being in this job, I see some strange stuff. You don't really know anyone, ever."

Her lips pressed together and she narrowed her gaze. "So should I trust you?"

He met her gaze. "You can, however..."

"Yes?" She asked.

Her eyes went wide and he wondered what she looked like when she orgasmed. Heat filled him. He shouldn't be thinking about that or contemplating touching her breasts or dreaming about licking his way down her body, tasting her.

"However what?"

He cleared his throat. "I probably shouldn't be trusted because honestly I'd like to tug you into a room where we were alone and do more than kiss you. That's why I'm not going to let us get into a situation where you'd be uncomfortable."

Pink darkened her cheeks as she leaned in. "Sometimes, uncomfortable is good."

He sucked in a breath as desire hit hard. The server stepped into the room with their plates. He didn't have time to say what he wanted to.

The food was wonderful, and Keeley let him have a bite of her burrito. It was filled with delicious beans and meat along with guacamole, a cheese sauce, some lettuce, tomatoes, onions, and something else that tasted of heaven.

"I love the food here. I can't come often, but when I do, I splurge. I think I've almost worked my way through the menu."

He blinked at her and smiled. "The whole menu?"

Her nose wrinkled as she nodded. "Yes, well not the drink or dessert menu, but most of the food. It's not a big menu, so it didn't take long, and honestly, my friends and I come here and order three meals between the four of us, and we split them. So I've had help going through the whole menu."

"Still it's impressive that you all are willing to chance eating something you don't like."

Her eyes twinkled. "But everything here is so good. They know how to cook."

"Are they from Mexico?"

She shrugged. "I don't know. I don't want to ask."

He nodded, understanding her hesitancy to talk about the subject. Señor Gonzalo tempted them with sweet treats, but Keeley said she was too full.

He wasn't ready to drop her off, and he didn't want to go down to the River Walk, so he turned to head to the place Cody had told him about. When he parked in the lot, her eyes were wide and full of merriment.

"We're going to play mini-golf." She might have even clapped her hands.

"Why not. I want to spend more time with you, and this is a wholesome activity."

Her eyes twinkled. "Very wholesome."

He opened his door and lifted his brows as he looked at her. "Don't open your door yet."

She rolled her eyes and shot him a sweet smile. "Since we're on a date, okay. But other times, I'm going to open my own door."

He laughed and hopped out, running around to help her out of from the car. She slid out and stood up. Because of the lot and where he'd parked, he'd stepped up to the sidewalk, which was much higher than he'd thought. They'd moved to the back of the car, and she was still at the lot level. She looked like a munchkin since she came up to just above his belly button.

Her gaze trailed up his body. The heat of her stare made his stomach tighten. He wanted her bad, but he wasn't going to push. This relationship needed to build naturally.

The sidewalk where he was standing was about a two-foot step up for her. Instead of making her step up, he hopped down. The smile she shot him sizzled in his belly.

"That's better," he said.

"I don't know." She lifted her eyebrows. "I liked the view."

He choked on his breath as laughter spilled out. "You did?"

Her lips quirked up, and she put her hand on his waist. "You are kind of good looking."

"Kind of?" He laughed as he led her closer to the building.

Her gaze shot to his, and she flashed him a broad smile. "I think I need more time and fewer clothes to give you a full run down."

Heat almost overwhelmed him. "Jesus, Keeley, that mouth of yours."

"This mouth knows plenty of tricks. But we're here at mini golf with loads of kids. Let's go play."

She pulled open the door and headed into the building. He followed, thinking this smart and sassy woman might just be exactly what he'd been looking for. She also had a smoking hot body with plenty of curves. But it was more than her curves and her looks, she was just plain fun to be with.

CHAPTER FIVE

Keeley stepped up to the counter, turning to look at Noah. His tongue swiped over his upper lip as his gaze traveled up her backside. When he saw she was looking at him, his face turned red. She'd caught him staring at her butt and maybe even liking it. Heat zipped up her spine.

She carried extra weight, but Noah didn't seem to mind. He positioned himself right beside her and placed his hand on her waist.

"The easy course or the difficult one?" he asked.

"Difficult, of course," she said as she lifted up and kissed his cheek.

His gaze heated, but the teenager working the counter came up and interrupted their flirting.

"Two for course two," Noah said.

"Sure thing. Would you like any water?" the guy behind the counter asked.

"Yes," Noah said. "We need water."

She handed the guy some money or tried to, but Noah

wouldn't allow her to pay. She put away her cash, thinking that she needed to be faster next time.

They grabbed their clubs, two balls, two bottles of water and headed out to play. The course wasn't packed, and there wasn't anyone behind them at the window to pay. They weren't in a rush.

He allowed her to go first. She set her bottle of water on the small table behind the t-box and approached the green. She drew in a deep breath and placed the ball then turned to look at Noah for a long second.

He seemed confident with himself. She'd been out with guys who had to win, or it would destroy everything they thought of themselves. Noah didn't seem that fragile. Maybe he wouldn't be able to take a loss to her, but if he was insecure, she should figure it out now. Her heart was already making plans for the future past this date. No, she would play like she usually did and see what type of person he really was.

"You want any pointers?" Noah asked.

She laughed then winked at him before turning her attention on the ball. She took in the length of the green. This mini-golf was decorated with cartoon characters in cowboy hats. There were obstacles in the shape of hotdogs, ice cream, and popcorn. Hole one looked easy. She adjusted and tapped the ball just right, sending it over the green, passed the chocolate ice cream cone and into the hole.

"Oh wow." Noah moved to her, surprise shining in his eyes. "Was that a lucky shot or are you an expert, and I should be glad I didn't place a bet on who would win?"

She turned to face him, the confidence of having played for years filling her. "On a real golf course I'm crap, but here, never bet against me."

He laughed then moved to her, kissing her nose. "So have you played golf then—you know, a big course with the carts, the drink ladies and a few drink men on those courses where the players aren't so insecure, the caddies, and everything else that goes with it?"

Noah set his ball on the tee box and lined up, hitting the ball close to the cup, but not sinking it.

"I've played a couple of times, but I don't have the swing to get the ball to the green."

"But you've been on the green before? So tell me..." Noah tapped the ball into the cup. "How are you once you get it to the green?"

"Almost perfect. If I can get it anywhere close to the cup, it's in."

Noah moved to her and his brows wrinkled. "I'm begging here. I need you to give me lessons. There's this annual golf tournament I participate in, and I need to get better. I hired a coach to help my long game, but he hasn't done anything for my green work."

She laughed as they moved to the second hole. "You're serious?"

"Yes, deadly. It's a huge rivalry thing, and I don't want to lose every year."

She lined up and took her shot, another hole in one. Noah shook his head as he placed his ball.

"I know it's petty, but I'm willing to be petty over this. A lot of the guys grew up playing. The closest I ever got to a golf game was chunking golf balls at cop cars."

He'd just hit his ball, and she stepped onto the green after it rolled past, putting up a hand to stop him.

"You threw golf balls at cops, and now you're like a mega-cop? What got you from your life of crime to this?"

Thinking of him as some punk who terrorized police officers was hard.

He chuckled and shook his head. "I grew up rough. I didn't have much. Actually, I had nothing. I stole tennis shoes — not because I wanted the latest, but mine didn't fit, hadn't for over a month."

"Wow, that sucks. As a child, I couldn't imagine going without."

She cracked open her bottle of water and took a sip before they moved on to the next hole. This one was easy too and she got another hole in one.

"I have to ask," Noah said. "How are you so good at this?"

She shrugged. "My life was the opposite of yours. At any one time, I probably owned ten pair of tennis shoes. Some years, I had like fifteen. I could wear each pair only twice a month. One year, I grew so fast I didn't even get to wear them all before I outgrew them."

His eyes stayed on her as he took a sip of water. He wiped his mouth with the back of his hand before he spoke. "But that doesn't explain the golf."

"My dad owned five of these places. I played all the time. It was easy babysitting for my parents after I turned eight or so. Every summer, I spent the entire summer playing mini-golf. I played so much that all the customers knew me by name. I eventually ended up teaching clinics for little kids. I felt sorry for the ones who couldn't hit the ball well at all."

His eyebrows crinkled. "So your family was rich?"

"Oh yes. The mini-golf thing was one of the smaller businesses. Dad owned a bunch of stuff, but because he owned mini-golf and I spent so much time on the courses, I saw a different side of life. Not harsh like yours, but I saw regular people. A lot of the other kids I went to school with didn't interact with regular people, ever."

He blinked his sweet blue eyes at her. "Regular people? What do you mean?"

She hit the ball for hole five, and this time it didn't go in on the first hit, mainly because this hole actually had real obstacles with a hidden cup. She stepped down the green, turning back to Noah to talk before she moved to her ball.

"It was private school. A lot of the kids ended up spending their time with nannies and at rich people camps, doing things like learning dressage and polo. Some of the camps were on yachts, and then there are the ones where they learn how to skydive, and rappel, and just a whole bunch of stuff rich kids do."

"Wait." He held up his hand with the ball and shook his head. "They have rich kid camps?"

"Sure. Did you ever do summer camp?" She hit the ball, sinking it on the second strike. It took Noah four hits to get the ball in the hole.

"No, I never did. We couldn't afford camp. I did go down to the Y during the summer for lunch. They had a free lunch program and the people who ran it, I think it was from church or something, also played basketball with us. They tried to make us feel like we weren't just poor kids begging for food. They also gave me extra sandwiches. That was good because usually I hadn't had anything to eat since the day before at lunch and I was starving."

She stared at him; her mouth open as she shook her head. "Shit, that sucks."

"It did, but it pushed me to stay in school. I met a group of agents when I was ten or so, still young enough to be impressed. They were doing something near my house, and I watched them for a while, then I was brave enough to ask them what they were doing after they busted a drug king in our neighborhood. The agent could have told me to bug off. Actually, that might have been the first thing she said, but then she took the time to tell me what the FBI was. When I asked how to get a job with the them, she took me over to a hamburger stand, bought me a burger and fries along with a coke—by the way, food was the way into my heart at the time because I was usually starving—and she laid it out. Told me what I needed to do. She asked me if I'd ever broken the law and I told her about the tennis shoes I'd taken. It was then that I learned about programs in the community to get free clothes. That talk kept me from working for the dealers on our street. I followed her advice and became an agent."

"Did you ever look her up and tell her how she influenced you?"

He shook his head as he placed his ball, a sad look on his face. "She died giving birth to her second child. There was a complication. The doctors couldn't save her."

"Oh man, that is terrible."

"Yes. I did send a letter to her husband and children, telling them how much of an impact she made in my life. They thanked me for keeping her memory alive." He glanced away and sighed. "Sorry, that was rather heavy."

Keeley's hand was on his arm, holding him in place. "Thank you for telling me. You're a good man."

He held her gaze for a moment. Then someone on the other course started yelling about getting a hole in one, and it broke the mood. The conversation turned light as they played through the next hole. She was having a great time with him. He was as good of a guy as she'd thought he was.

"So your dad's businesses, what happened?" Noah asked as they started on hole twelve.

"Well, the man I thought could do no wrong was doing a lot of wrong. He was embezzling money that he was laundering. The mini-golf business was how he washed the dirty money."

Noah's lips thinned before he answered. "Money laundering, that's some nasty stuff."

"Yes. I was at school in New York. Columbia like you."

"Wow. We weren't there at the same time, though? Right? I mean, you're younger than me."

She laughed and turned to him, thinking this guy really was sexy. If she'd seen him on campus, she would have chased after him. "I was there four years ago."

"Okay, then no. I graduated with my masters eight years ago. I've been with the FBI since then." He moved close and plucked a leaf from her hair before closing the distance. His lips slid over hers in a sweet kiss.

She blinked up at him, wishing they were in private so she could explore that kiss deeper. His touch felt like a thousand suns. The heat coursing through her was almost too much, and she welcomed the breeze that came after.

"So tell me about leaving Columbia," he said.

"I was in the first semester of my second year when I got the call. My dad had been arrested. It all came crashing down on him hard. He lost all of his businesses, the house, the beach house. Yes, we owned a beach house in Padre and many expensive cars. My Kia was the least expensive car we owned, and because he'd put it in my name, I didn't lose it. Basically, he screwed up."

"That's rough. So what happened?"

"I finished the last three weeks of school and tried to book a ticket home for winter break, but there was no money. My credit cards had been cut off, and then I tried my bank. I had twenty dollars left to my name. I'd never been poor or hungry. At Columbia, my parents had paid for full dining, so I didn't feel the pinch until school was over."

"I guess that's good. How long were you in New York after the semester ended?"

She took a sip of her water, her mind clouding. "Since I'd left my car in Texas, I had no easy way to get home. I ended up begging for money so I could eat. I wasn't prepared for it at all. I tried to make a go at staying in New York, but I couldn't get an apartment, I couldn't even rent a room. I lived in the subway for a week, but that was dangerous."

He swallowed hard, worry filling his face. "You weren't attacked, were you?"

The shadows over her thoughts increased. That had been such a difficult time. "There was one night I thought I was going to be, but I ran and got away."

"I'm glad you escaped." Noah finished out hole fifteen, and she placed her ball for the next hole. There wasn't anyone else around, so she felt comfortable telling the rest of the story.

"I woke up one afternoon so hungry I thought I might have killed for a sandwich. I decided that day to sell my body for money, so I could at least afford a hot meal. It was scary. The men buying women aren't like you, they were different."

He stepped closer to her and put his hand on her shoulder. "I've been on details with the FBI where we've been in those areas. I know what you're talking about."

She sucked in air through her nose as pain filled her heart. It had been difficult living like that. She wanted to continue the story because talking to Noah felt good. "I couldn't go through with it. It was too much to ask. Instead, I begged for money, stole some from unsuspecting people, and got enough to make it home. I hitchhiked south as far as Columbia, South Carolina. Then I bought a ticket on Greyhound to make it the rest of the way. Actually the trucker I hitched with had a daughter my age, he paid for half the ticket. He would have driven me the whole way, but he was headed to Florida and only took a detour to Columbia to get me on a bus. I showed up in San Antonio the day after Christmas. Of course, we didn't have a home left. Dad and Mom were in jail. Turns out she was in on it too."

"That's rough." Noah turned serious. "You didn't know anything?"

"No. I was stupid back then or maybe they hid it well. I had absolutely no clue they were doing anything illegal. It made sense though."

He cocked his head to the side. "Why do you say that?"

"Their fights. I really had no clue and I just thought they were fighting. Now that I'm an adult and understand money better, I know more about what those fights were about. I didn't understand it back then."

"Do you still see them?" he asked.

"A few times a year. It's weird. I mean they are my parents, but after everything fell apart, they weren't the same. They were rude, like I've never seen them that rude. I tried, but after a few times getting yelled at, I gave up going every week, then I gave up going every month. I write, but they still seem bitter that I'm out here and they are in jail."

They were on the eighteenth hole, and she didn't want the evening to end this way. She drew in a shaky breath as she lined up to hit the ball. Before she tapped the ball, she turned to him.

"I don't want our night to end with me telling this shitty story." She tossed her empty water bottle in the recycle bin.

Noah nodded. "Let's go for some ice cream or something. I don't want this night to end either. But please tell me what you did." Noah finished his water and threw it in the bin too.

She shrugged. "I lived in a shelter for a few nights, got cleaned up, and went begging for friends to help. They all knew what my dad had done, and no one would help me except one guy whose father owned a fast-food restaurant. I got a job flipping burgers. Everyone turned their back on me. I eventually got certified to be a dental assistant, mainly because I got a grant for school."

"So you didn't want to be a dental assistant?" Noah asked as he took the club and led her over to the window to return their equipment.

"Anyone get a hole in one?" the attendant asked.

Noah and her both burst out laughing. "She got a few," Noah called over his shoulder as he led her inside the building. After they used the restroom, they headed across the street to an ice cream shop.

Once they were in the lot, he started asking questions again. "So if you weren't a dental assistant, what would you do?"

The loss of her dream still made her ache. "I don't know."

"Sure, you do. You were going to school for something."

She looked at the ice cream, thinking about her past, how naïve she'd been. There were signs her father wasn't on the up and up when she'd been growing up, but she hadn't cared enough to pay attention.

"What can I get you?" the girl behind the counter asked.

"Single scoop of chocolate," Keeley said.

"I'll have a single of butter pecan."

"Sure."

She insisted that she pay for the ice cream, and Noah let her. They took a seat in the far corner her mind on what her future could have been.

"So, what would you have done?"

"I was studying art history. I had dreams of working at a museum. Of course, at the time I figured I had a huge trust fund backing me up."

"If you could, would you go back and get an art history degree?"

"Yes," she answered before she could stop the words. They hurt to say. She would give up her job, her paycheck to get back into art.

He nodded and licked off more ice cream. No other man had ever asked her what her dreams for her life were. They just assumed she was doing what she wanted to do. She liked Doc Julian, and her job wasn't bad, but it wasn't her dream job or even close to it.

"So you're in your dream job," Keeley stated. "I'm not sure I could make it to mine."

He shrugged. "You're young, and even if you weren't, you could still do it."

She ate some more ice cream, thinking about how her life would change.

"I don't know. I would have to quit work, find a new job to cover expenses, get a loan, or a scholarship. It would be a lot."

He nodded. "I waited tables for two years to get enough money to pay for college. I understand the sacrifices."

She licked at her ice cream, sadness skirting the sides of her mind. "I don't know that I'm the type of person who is strong enough to do that."

He took a long lick of his ice cream before he leaned forward, and his voice went low. "I've seen a lot of crazy shit in my time as an FBI agent. Do you know how many people ruin their lives after something happens to them that's really out of their control? There are so many people behind bars not because they were born into crime, but they make a choice when life got hard. Your life got hard."

She shrugged. "It doesn't compare to yours."

He shook his head. "It may have been worse. I grew up poor, living next to crack dens. I saw how terrible it could be and found a rope to pull myself out with. You were given everything, and life crapped on you. You weren't given a rope as a lifeline, you were given a noose to hang yourself."

She licked at her melting ice cream before responding. "What do you mean?"

"Your friends turned their back on you. Your parents took away the safety net. You were left alone and without a way to get back up. So many people make a choice to sell their bodies or deal drugs or some other life of crime that is devastating. They don't turn their lives around."

She licked her cone, pushing the ice cream beneath the top of the cone before she pulled it away and stared at it; his words wrapping around her thoughts, making her feel weird about some of the choices she'd made.

"I did give up, though."

"How so?" he asked.

"I don't want to work at a dentist office. I hate having to look in other people's mouths. It's not what I want to do."

"So how can I help you?"

She dropped her hand and stared at Noah over their melting ice cream. "You want to help me? But you don't know me."

The look in his eyes made her want to throw herself at him and wrap her arms around his neck and cry, but she didn't move.

"I'm sure there are ways I can help. I may not be able to do much, but what if we went looking at colleges around here this weekend."

She swallowed, thinking about all the negative things she'd said about schools here. Those ideas were bread through elitism and fostered by peers who enjoyed taking stabs at the locals. Of course, they'd taken their stabs at her and her daddy for owning mini-golf places. It hadn't stopped them from begging for free games.

"I was a little shit growing up."

Noah chuckled as he finished his ice cream then wiped his hands with the napkin. "So was I. I mean I threw golf balls at cop cars."

She laughed. "Why did you do that?"

"We were bored, and it was summer. One of the kids in the neighborhood was working at a golf course on the other side of town. They brought home a bucket of balls, and there was a riot in our neighborhood. I went up to the roof of a building, and we started chunking golf balls when they threw tear gas into the group. We were little shits."

She shook her head. "How did you not get arrested?"

"I don't know. I mean now, when I see people do stupid shit to cops, I get pissed. I did it, but it still pisses me off." Noah reached over to the nearby counter and grabbed a couple of packs of wet wipes to clean their hands. "The cops had their hands full that day. They'd shot a four-year-old who was holding a toy knife. The cop said he feared for his life and shot the little kid. It turned our city over. I was six at the time and didn't know any better."

"That's awful."

"Yeah. The cop lost his job, was sent to jail, served five years, and got out. Someone found out where he was living and shot him. They never figured out who killed him."

"That is terrible."

"It is. But he shouldn't have been a cop in the first place. If a four-year-old holding a toy made him feel threatened, he didn't deserve to be on the force."

She nodded then shook her head. "It's rough. So do you get put into positions like that, where the situation is a tough call?"

"Yes. But we train a lot. I shoot every week, and then my reaction gets tested in stressful situations over and over again. We can't afford to make a mistake. If I shoot someone, it has to be clean."

"So have you shot someone?"

He nodded as his eyes clouded. "Being an agent means making tough choices. I can't tell you what we did today, but it was rough for a few hours."

"At work we were talking about stuff downtown being blocked because of a shooting, was that you guys?"

He gave a slight nod, and she guessed he didn't want to talk about it. She didn't blame him. His life was so different than hers.

Noah glanced down at his watch. "Oh gosh, it's late. I should get you home."

She stood and placed a hand on his chest. Their gazes met and held, something deep passing between them.

"Thank you for talking and going out with me. It was nice to have this be more than a session for you to gage how to get into my pants."

He chuckled and leaned in, his lips were right by her ear, sending shivers down her spine.

"I like you as a person, and I'm still a guy who likes women. I wouldn't mind being in your pants right now, but I want us to last for more than a few dates." His finger trailed over her shoulder and down her arm. "This thing between us, I know it's new, but Keeley, I like you."

She shivered as she lifted her chin, adjusting so their lips brushed together. The kiss was short, sweet, but she felt it all the way to her toes. Noah moaned and didn't move away.

"You're tempting me," he said.

She backed up and gave him a wry smile. "Like you aren't tempting me."

He chuckled and took her arm, leading her out to the car. This date had been the best she'd ever had. No man had ever cared enough to ask about what she wanted or cared enough to listen to how her past had changed her. Some guys wanted to find out if her dad still had money, and others just didn't care. Noah was different. This could end up being a fantastic relationship, that was if she didn't blow it. It had been ages since she'd actually dated and she really wanted to see Noah again, but she didn't want to appear too eager.

She glanced over, catching his profile, thinking this man probably had no clue he was way out of her league. She had a job, she lived in her own apartment, but she was barely making it. Would he dump her once he figured out having dreams of more was beyond the scope of her capabilities? She would never get ahead. Her father had seen to that when he'd taken her last dime and left her penniless.

CHAPTER SIX

NOAH WISHED HE'D BEEN DATING KEELEY FOR WEEKS or months so when he pulled up at her place he could have stayed. He wanted to sleep with her, but more than the sex, he wanted her to be safe. She lived in a terrible neighborhood. Earlier he thought it was bad, then when he'd dropped her, he saw five different drug deals going down. She didn't fit in here and shouldn't live in this rat trap. Of course, he had no right to tell her she couldn't stay. He would come across as some Neanderthal dickweasel.

He needed to check how much support the San Antonio police gave the citizens of this neighborhood. From what he knew of the city, it wasn't much. Though he didn't think the area was safe, he hadn't heard one gunshot. No gun violence meant the cops wouldn't show. They were busy in other areas where life was even more dangerous than it was here.

He gave her a short and sweet kiss goodnight, then left. Walking away had been difficult.

Once home, he stripped out of his clothes and hopped into the shower. The day had been long and hot, but he was happy to have spent time with Keeley. She was smart, sexy, and fun to be with. Their talk had turned serious, and he felt like he knew her better now. They'd grown up so differently. She'd had everything handed to her then ripped away, and he'd had to fight for everything he had.

He ran the soap down his body, his thoughts on Keeley and her gorgeous mouth. An image of her on her knees, her lips wrapped around his cock filled his mind. He needed to get to know her better before they had sex. The last thing he wanted was for her to get the wrong message from him and he'd found pushing sex too early in a relationship tended to lead to crossed wires. It had ended more relationships too soon for him than he cared to admit.

For now, his hand would do. He let the images of Keeley play through his mind. Her lips were full and her ass was too. It would feel so good to pump into her from behind. He came hard as he imagined her bent over in front of him.

Before he stretched out, he sent a note to his boss about Keeley and how her parents were in jail. He didn't think it would be a problem since she'd been young when they'd done their illegal activity, and she had little contact with them now.

He drifted off to thoughts about her. The next day at work was good. When he texted Keeley a little after noon, he didn't expect a reply, but she said she was on lunch break. He wanted to see her again but kept things light and asked if she wanted to get together on Saturday to look at universities in the area. She agreed, and they set the time for nine on Saturday morning.

The rest of his week went smoothly, and on Saturday, he was ready to see Keeley. He pulled up outside her apartment, and she rushed out before he had a chance to open his door. He hopped out quickly and met her on the sidewalk. His arms went around her and pulled her close. She smelled of fresh shampoo and mouthwash, and he took a chance and brushed his lips over hers. The kiss sent sparks through him. If this was how he reacted when they kissed, he was in for a hot time when they had sex.

"You ready?" he asked.

"Yes. I'm caffeinated and full. Let's go."

"Awesome. So the first place I thought we would look at is the University of Texas local campus. The place isn't too far from here, and they have an art history major."

"Wow, I'm impressed," Keeley said as he held the passenger door for her.

"I take my job seriously." He chuckled, not wanting to tell her that there was only one art history program in San Antonio.

It took them about fifteen minutes to drive over since the traffic was light. He parked near the admissions building, and they walked over to a group of young people, maybe high school age, that had formed in front of the building.

"What is going on?" Keeley asked.

He couldn't help but smile. He'd found out they had tours on Saturdays at this time of year and thought it would be a great way for her to see the campus and get an idea of what she wanted to do.

He lifted his brows. "It's a tour."

"You knew there was a tour?"

His heart skipped a beat at the look on her face. "Yes. I found out they had one this morning and I wasn't sure if we would make it, but I'm glad we did."

She pulled him close and gave him a huge hug. "Thank you."

Her lips landed on his cheek, and pleasure rippled through him. Making her happy thrilled him. He wanted to keep doing things to make her happy because seeing her eyes light up brought joy to him.

The tour started, and they walked along the central area of the campus. The stuff about dorms wasn't necessary to her, but they also pointed out the city bus schedule connecting the university with the rest of San Antonio. They had information about each college, and they found out there was an art show in the Main Gallery in the art building later in the day.

Once the tour ended, Keeley picked up a packet of information, and they headed over to a restaurant just off-campus. No one else was in the dining room, and they had their choice of seats so he led her to a booth where they'd be hidden. He slid in beside her, liking how her knee touched his.

"Are you excited about returning to studies?"

She nodded. "I am, but there's no way I can afford to go here."

"Maybe you could take a couple of classes. I know it seems impossible, but if you start chipping away at it, eventually you'll have your degree."

She sighed and flipped a page in the brochure. "I don't know. It's so much money."

"They have a master's in art history."

"They do." She swallowed hard, looking a little depressed. "It's no Columbia."

"No, but it is the University of Texas. The school has a good name."

Their food arrived, and she closed the material and set it aside. "So how was your week?"

"Good. We made a few big arrests. I ended up on the coast on Thursday and yesterday."

"Really? How was the beach?"

"Hot." He picked up his fork and knife then cut off a bite of food. "Also we didn't hit the beach. I was in the San Bernard National Wildlife Refuge. Because they were in a national park, I was able to make the arrest. Now they have a federal crime charged against them."

She cut her eyes his way, a smirk forming on her lips. "So you were in the Texas swamps."

He chuckled. "I was. We saw a few gators and a bobcat."

"Wow, that's so weird. And now here you are, in the middle—well, nearly suburb—of a city, being all civilized and stuff."

Laughter struck hard. When he recovered, he cupped her behind the neck and held her in place as he kissed her, his tongue licking at her lips. She opened, and he deepened the kiss, wishing they were at his place. He heard footsteps shuffling behind them and ended the kiss, sitting up just as the waiter came around the corner of the booth.

"Would you like more to drink?"

"No thank you," Keeley said.

"We're good," Noah said. "Thank you."

They were done eating and still had thirty minutes before the art show started. After he paid, they walked out to the campus and wandered around the buildings. He led her to the area where the show would take place and pulled out his phone.

"I think you should start the application process now."

"What?" She looked shocked.

"You can create an account and save your progress. Then later tonight, you can finish filling it out."

She drew in a deep breath and shrugged. "Might as well. Do you mind?"

"No. Here, take my phone and start."

The form was easy. In less than twenty minutes she'd filled out half the application and saved her progress.

"I'm ready to go in now." She stood and handed the phone back to Noah. "Thank you for encouraging me to do this."

"Of course, I'm excited for you." He liked how bright her eyes looked now. She was a changed woman, like maybe she had hope. He had thought she was beautiful before, now she radiated happiness.

The gallery was on the second floor of the art building and was full of people. He was surprised by how many people were here. During his time at Columbia he didn't think he would have wasted a Saturday. But these people didn't look like they thought their time was being wasted.

Keeley seemed entranced by a few of the paintings. She was staring at one for a long time. He liked watching her. Her expression changed a little the more she looked at the art, like maybe she'd unlocked some secret code. He had to know.

"What do you think is so special about this one?" he asked.

She glanced at him, her eyes full of happiness. Her excitement thrilled him. "If you look at the way it's painted, it reminds me of Picasso's early work."

"Isn't he the dude that did the cube stuff?" He didn't know much about art, not really, but this didn't look anything like the Picasso stuff he'd seen.

"Yes, but Picasso did so much more than cubist art. He had a huge career, painting thousands of pieces. He was an amazing artist. There is so much to him. So much history and you have to look at history to understand what the artists were going through. Now then, is this young artist copying Picasso because Picasso became famous, or is the artist going through difficult times?"

Noah leaned in, staring at the painting. "How can you tell?"

"There's so much that can be ferreted out with art." Her words sped up and her voice seemed a little higher. "See how the leg is bent on this man?"

"Yes," Noah said.

"Well, the original painting from Picasso has the man's leg outstretched. He's moving forward, this man's leg is back, stalled. The woman is the one moving forward. She's reaching for the child, whereas in Picasso's painting she's attached to the man. They are one, in love in Picasso's work, but this couple doesn't look in love. Instead, they look like their world is falling apart. And the woman holding the baby seems to be taking the baby, instead of just holding it."

"Wow." He narrowed his eyes, squinting as he studied the people in the painting. "You can tell all of that from a painting?"

"Yes." Keeley moved to the next painting. "This is by the same artist. They have another sad painting about a baby. It's being kept from its parents. I'm guessing she or someone she knows lost a baby, and this is how she mourns for it."

He shook his head. "That's sad."

"It is." Keeley turned to face him. "Life is full of disappointments."

"She's right," an older gentleman stepped up, his hand outstretched. "I'm Professor Dunwitty. Are you one of our students?"

Keeley took his hand for a shake. "Professor Dunwitty, I'm not enrolled yet."

"But she's going to," Noah said.

"Master's program?" Dunwitty asked.

"No, sir. I had to drop out my sophomore year. So I'll be undergraduate. My goal is a master's in art history, but it will take forever."

"Young lady, it will only take forever if you don't start. It may seem daunting, but your knowledge of Picasso is impressive. I was listening to you. I would love to have you in a class and hear your take on other masters and what they were facing at the time. You're right, art is more than just pretty stuff to look at, it's the history of our world through the eyes of one person, mixed with the history of their lives. It's real, devastating at times, and provocative."

Keeley turned to the paintings and nodded. "I want to come here. Talking to you has encouraged me, but I have to figure out a few things."

"Finances?" Dunwitty asked.

She sighed, and her lips turned down. "Yes. I don't have any money for school."

"I have just the thing." Dunwitty held up his finger and told them to stay put.

"So what do you think?" Noah asked. He felt encouraged by Dunwitty's words. Maybe there was another way he could help Keeley.

"I'm excited. Talking to him about art made me excited like I used to be. Art is thrilling."

Dunwitty came around the corner and held out a pamphlet. "This is the school's scholarship pamphlet. There are scholarships for people who are returning to school. I would encourage you to fill these out, all of them that apply, and get moving on it. I would love to have you in my class. It would be exciting to discuss artists with you."

"Thank you, sir." Keeley clutched the pamphlet, looking like she would never let it go. He liked the excitement he saw in her eyes.

"Well, I'd best be moving on. I have to talk to my students who have shown up. They are only here because I'm giving them two points credit. Funny how that works."

Keeley thanked Dunwitty again then turned to Noah after the professor walked off. She gave him a quick hug and pulled back fast.

"Oh my goodness, I could actually go here."

His heart rate picked up. "I'm excited for you."

"Thank you for bringing me here. I can't believe this has been so close and I never came over here to check it out."

He couldn't help but laugh. "I think this is the perfect time."

She cocked her head to the side, and her nose wrinkled. "Really, why?"

"Well, running into Dunwitty can't have been a mistake."

"No, I guess not." Her face scrunched up as her eyes went unfocused for a moment. "It's weird, since meeting you my life just keeps getting better and better."

He leaned in, his lips at her ear. "Maybe because we were meant to be together."

She laughed and wrapped her arm around his waist. He nuzzled her ear and she moaned. He heated and stepped back. This wasn't the time or the place to get more intimate. They finished looking at the rest of the paintings, not spending as long on the other ones. When they stepped outside, the sun was covered by clouds, but it wasn't raining. He didn't want to drop her off at her house, but he had work he needed to accomplish.

"Today was great, thank you," Keeley said.

"It was. I hope we can see each other on Wednesday or Thursday this week." He couldn't hide his desire to see her. Maybe his life would get in the way, or hers, but he honestly just wanted her by his side.

"Come over on Wednesday, and I'll cook you dinner."

Her words filled him with longing. It had been ages since anyone had cooked him a meal. "You don't have to cook for me."

Her smile was electric. "I want to."

"Okay, what time?"

"Six on Wednesday. Anything you would love to have?"

He shook his head. He couldn't make her do something special for him. "I'll eat anything."

Her lips quirked up. "Okay, I can do that."

Her confidence filled him with joy. Keeley was going to cook for him. It had been a long time since someone had done that. He liked how she made him feel special. He wanted to spend more time with her.

The drive to her apartment went by too quickly. Noah walked her to her door, making sure she locked up before he drove away. Again, he felt the menace of the area. Maybe he could help her search for a new place to live. Somewhere the crime stats were less troublesome. Paranoia filled him, sending tingles down his spine. There was something off about the area, and he didn't like it. He wanted Keeley to be safe, which he wasn't sure was possible in this neighborhood.

CHAPTER SEVEN

KEELEY PLOPPED DOWN ON HER BED AND HUGGED HER pillow. Spending the day with Noah had been amazing. His eyes were so expressive and full of kindness. He'd taken her to the university and shown her how wonderful her life could be. She needed to make this happen.

After a moment, she hopped up, grabbed her computer, and started filling out forms for scholarships. She'd filled out two and believed she had a good chance of getting some help. She'd started on the third form when her neighbor began banging on the wall. She needed peace and quiet, and from past experience, she knew this type of behavior could go on for hours. She packed up her computer, grabbed a protein bar and a bottle of water, and headed out to Doc Julian's office. He didn't mind her being in the office if she cleaned up.

She keyed in and locked the door behind her, then turned off the alarm. She set up in the break room so no one walking past would think they were open. After she finished filling out the application to attend the university, there were forms for five more scholarships she had to fill out. It would take her hours, but what else was she going to do.

A little after the sun went down, she ate the protein bar and drank her water. She was getting tired, but she was almost done. She'd filled out the form to register to attend and didn't believe she'd be rejected. Her grades had been excellent through high school and in Columbia.

The last form she had to fill out required an essay. She was busy writing when she heard something in the front of the office. She ignored it, thinking it had to be someone outside making noise. She turned back to the form, forcing herself to concentrate when she heard voices. They weren't distant. Instead, they were inside the office. Tingles made her spine stiff as she gasped for a breath.

She sat up and bumped into the table, almost knocking over her water. Righting the bottle, she closed her laptop and scrambled to do something, but she wasn't sure what.

Fear shot through her, sending a load of adrenaline with it. She turned just as a guy stepped around the corner. Dread filled her. The man wore a plaid shirt and old jeans with brown boots. He looked rough with a scraggly beard and dark eyes. Her heart sped up as reality sunk in. She was alone, and these strangers had her trapped.

"What do you want?" her voice was squeaky and shook.

"What's ours. That's what we want," the man barked.

Another guy walked around the corner and headed to the sink, opening the cabinet. "It's gone." The guy turned and stalked toward her. She backed up, trying to escape him, but he kept coming. "Where are the packages?"

Her hands were shaking, and her knees felt weak. "I don't have what you want."

"Well, then you'd better find it," the first guy said.

"I-I can't." She fumbled in her pocket, praying she could dial 911 without them noticing.

The guy reached into her pocket and grabbed her phone, flinging it across the room. The sound of glass smashing made her heart stop. A whimper escaped her lips. She had no way to contact anyone. She was going to die.

"Grab her. We'll use her as a bargaining chip," the first guy said.

"What if they don't return the cocaine?" one of the guys asked.

"Then she'd better be a fucking good whore because we'll use her to make our money back."

"No!" Keeley yelled, but the men only laughed. The first guy grabbed her, holding her close. She fought hard, pulling her hands away from him, but it was no use. The guy wound up his arm and popped her in the side of the head with his fist. The world went fuzzy, and she dropped to her knees.

"Pick her up and bring her with us. We'll figure out what to do later."

Keeley tried screaming, but it was no use. There was no one here, no one in the offices nearby, and they didn't have cameras. She'd lost her phone and had no way to contact the cops or Noah.

Oh God, Noah.

He would never find out what happened to her. He would just assume she'd ghosted him. A sob escaped her lips as she was tossed into the trunk of a car. The trunk lid slammed shut, locking her in.

She wanted to fight, wanted to escape, but her head swam, and her arms felt heavy. There was no escape. At least she'd found out who had brought in the drugs, and it wasn't anyone from her work. The thought made more tears come. She hadn't been at risk by those who worked with her. Instead, it was just some random fluke Doc Julian hired guys to fix the window who were drug dealers too. Now she was paying the price for her boss going with someone who the insurance company hadn't vetted.

CHAPTER EIGHT

P<small>AIN HIT FIRST, THEN SHE OPENED HER EYES AND SAW</small> nothing. Fear took hold, ratcheting up the panic. A steady hum grew as she gained consciousness. Then she felt movement and knew she was in the back of a car. Oh God, she was in the trunk of a car being taken to God only knows where. No one would ever find her.

Tears fell, and she wiped them away, forcing a calm she didn't feel. At least they hadn't tied her hands. She felt around, searching for a way to escape the trunk, but there wasn't anything to grab or pull. She was stuck.

The calm she'd achieved threatened to be dashed when the tire noise changed. Were they going to pull her out and kill her, or worse, just fill the trunk full of bullet holes? She didn't want to die this way. The trunk of this car wasn't what she wanted her final resting place to be.

More tears came and then grew when the car stopped. Noah would never know she was beginning to fall in love with him. Keeley didn't have a great relationship with her dad, but she didn't hate him. She felt the same way about her mom. She just wanted the chance to say goodbye.

Leaving this way, dying in the trunk of some car, wasn't how she wanted to go.

A sharp click was followed by the trunk opening. She let out a squeak as she stared up into the faces of the men who'd taken her. One of them bent to pick her up, but she lashed out trying to keep his hands off her.

"Bitch, don't scratch me."

The punch came fast, stunning her. Her head spun, and her body heated. Her nose felt like it was ballooning. Had they broken it?

The guy picked her up and threw her over his shoulder. His hands were on her ass as he carried her up a set of stairs to a porch. They were taking her into a house. She looked up, trying to figure out where they were. It was dark. There was one light in the distance. That was all she could see because trees and bushes surrounded the area. Everything was black. Was that a house next door? Was she even in San Antonio?

"Where do you want her?" the guy carrying her asked someone.

"Third room." The sound of the reply didn't make her feel any better. She was someone's captive now.

Doors were opened, and she was taken upstairs. The click of locks being thrown told her whatever door they were opening wasn't going to be easy to break free from. Another door was open. She chanced a glance in, seeing four young girls, mostly naked, huddled together on a mattress. Shocked pulsed through her.

The guy carrying her lowered her then she fell about three feet, landing with a hard thunk. A foot came out of nowhere, kicking her in the ribs. She cried out then curled into a ball, more tears flowing. Her ankle was jerked hard. Cold hands were on her legs.

"She'll get a good price." The scratchy old voice sent chills through her. "She's got tits and that ass. Guys like to pound that shit."

"Might have a go before we sell her." Laughter erupted around the room.

"You know Donald doesn't like it when you sample the merch." The scratchy voice was still close. A hand ran up her leg. She tried jerking away, but her leg was grabbed and pulled back. Something cold wrapped around her ankle.

"Donald can suck my dick."

"He'll chop it off," Scratchy Voice barked, the agitation evident.

"Won't do no such thing."

Someone grabbed her hair and pulled her up. Pain raced down her neck, shocking her. She opened her mouth to scream. Her face was shoved against some guy's crotch, rough denim scratching her lips. She tried to fight, but the man was stronger than her. He yanked her head back painfully, forcing her to look up at him. His yellow stained teeth sat under a thick mustache.

"You'll suck me. Just wait. Then I'm going to rape your ass."

She wanted to tell him she'd never sleep with him, but she had little doubt this man could force her. He let go by flinging her head back. She crashed to the ground, her skull thumping on the plywood floor.

The three of them left, flipping off the lights as they went. The sound of the locks clicking into place crushed her soul. They'd shackled her to the floor. She was locked in a room, in a house in the middle of somewhere that she didn't know. The place was being guarded by an asshole with a scratchy voice and who knows who else. She would never escape. She curled up tight, tears making her eyes burn.

"Quit yer crying." The voice was small, feminine, and young sounding. She also sounded very country.

Keeley jerked her head up, searching for the person who had spoken.

"Over 'er. Don't think you can make it over, least the last girl they had in here couldn't."

Keeley wiped the back of her hand across her nose, sniffling as she tried to sit up. Pain filled her, and she let out a little gasp.

"His boot hurts," the woman said. "You learn to just shut it and take it."

"Take what?" Keeley's voice shook.

"The sex, stupid. It's over quick. They don't last long. It's not like porn where all those guys take Viagra and other pills to keep it up. That dude, he's about two minutes max, actually more like thirty seconds, but I'd never tell him. He thinks he's great. His cock is big, though. Hurts like a mother fucker."

A sob racked Keeley's body. She pulled her knees in tighter, wrapping her arm around them.

"You owe them money?" the stranger asked.

"No. I mean, I guess they think I do. I don't know."

"Well, if someone will pay a ransom, don't expect to go home without being raped a few times. The last girl they had in here, her daddy was rich. She got it bad. Not sure he paid."

"Last girl?"

"Yup," the girl said. "The bitch was seventeen. By the time they finished with her, she looked forty."

The turn of a key in the locks made Keeley's heart race. She scooted as far away from the door as she could, praying they weren't coming in for her. Maybe they were bringing food or water. Or maybe someone was rescuing her.

Light spilled in, blinding her for a few seconds. Someone stepped into the room. Luckily for her, they went for the other woman. The laugh from the stranger who shared her prison sent a shiver down Keeley's spine.

"Let's go, baby," the strange woman yelled as she was led out.

Keeley watched, trying to get a good look at the woman, but there wasn't enough light. All Keeley could tell was the woman was skinny, looking like maybe she'd been starved. The door slammed. Keeley was thrilled she hadn't been taken but immediately felt guilty.

The quiet only lasted for a moment, then Keeley heard grunting and groaning. The noise was over soon, then started back up. That happened three times. She guessed there were three guys downstairs.

Tears ran down Keeley's face. Her life as she knew it was over. The hopes of getting her art degree were gone. She should have tried earlier. Living like she had for the last few years had shown the defeat she felt in her soul. Long ago, before her father lost everything, she'd been happy and filled with hope. When she'd been forced to come home from Columbia, she'd given up her dreams. Why had she allowed fear to rule her?

Sure, it would be hard to go to school and work. She would have to study, and her life would change, but once she graduated and got a job in the museum or art world, it would be worth all the pain. Now that chance was gone. She'd waited too late and ruined her life through inaction.

The door opened, sending fear through Keeley. The woman was tossed in then chained to the floor. She didn't move. While the door was open, the light spilling in, Keeley searched the corners of the room. There was a bucket close to where her chain was bolted in. No sinks, no other water source. This was a bare-bones room without any amenities.

Keeley shivered, knowing deep down what that bucket was for. She wouldn't make it out of here alive, and if she were sold, the hell she would find had to be ten times worse. The door shut, and locks were thrown, imprisoning her in this cell that was her new life.

CHAPTER NINE

Keeley didn't return Noah's text on Sunday. He wanted to see her and drove to her place late in the afternoon, but she didn't answer the door. Honestly, he didn't know her well. She was intriguing, beautiful, sweet, kind, smart, all the things he wanted in a partner. It was scary to think he could have found 'the one.'

On Monday morning when he arrived at work, she still hadn't returned his text, so he called as he was walking into the building. The phone clicked, indicating she'd answered. He was about to say something cute when a male voice drew him up sharp.

"Who is this?" The question was harsh and to the point. Fear spiked as possibilities exploded through his mind.

"Special Agent Noah Grey of the FBI based in San Antonio. Who is this?"

"Officer Deaver of the San Antonio Police Department. How do you know Miss Anderson?"

"I'm dating her," Noah sputtered.

"Sir, I'm at Doctor Julian Davenport's office. There was

a break-in, and Miss Anderson's phone, computer, and bag are here. I need you to come over right away."

"Shit, have you put out an APB for her?"

"Sir, if you could come here and answer a few questions," Deaver said.

His stomach twisted. Of course, he was going to be a person of interest. Someone walked past then turned back to him. It was Cody. His face was screwed up with worry. Noah drew in a deep breath and held up one finger, hoping Cody stuck around. He needed to have someone on his side. This could go south fast.

"I'll be there in a few."

He ended the call, pain filling him. There was little doubt in his mind Keeley had been abducted. He drew in a slow breath and met Cody's gaze.

"What's wrong?" Cody asked.

"Keeley has disappeared."

"What?"

"The woman I've been dating." Noah raked his hand through his hair. "We spent Saturday together. I dropped her off that afternoon. I texted her on Sunday and didn't hear anything. I even went by her place and knocked. I just thought she was out, you know, maybe shopping or something. Then I called this morning. A police officer answered her phone. They said her purse, phone, and computer were found at the dentist office where she works. They want me to come over for questioning."

Cody held up one hand. "You didn't have anything to do with her disappearance?"

The question was a punch to Noah's gut. "No. Of course, you don't know me. We just met, but no. No way would I ever do that."

"Okay." Cody's lips thinned. "We need to head over. I'm calling my boss and who are you under?"

"Jessica Long. I'll call her now."

"Good, good." Cody was on the phone, talking to his boss, and Noah called Special Agent Long and got her voice mail.

"It's Agent Noah Grey. I need you to call me. The woman I've been dating has gone missing. I'm headed over to talk to the cops right now. Agent Cody Whittaker is with me."

He ended the call, hating that he had to go in for questioning. But the sooner they eliminated him, the faster they could move on to searching for the real killers.

"You ready?" Cody asked him.

"Let's go."

They took Cody's car because he knew there was the possibility he would be taken downtown. The statistics weren't in his favor. Most murders and abductions were conducted by a person the victim knew. He guessed the cops were salivating over the fact they might catch a G-Man for murder. He was happy to disappoint them. There wasn't any way they could reasonably pin this murder on him, but small-town cops weren't always reasonable. And while San Antonio wasn't a small town, the police working the scene could have a small-town mentality.

It took them fifteen minutes to get there. Long called and insisted she come to the scene too. Noah had reluctantly given over the address. When they pulled up, he noticed Keeley's car had finally been towed. Everything looked back to normal, and all evidence of the tornado was gone except the dip in the grass where the tree had been ripped up and deposited on Keeley's vehicle.

"You ready for this?" Cody asked.

He fisted his hands. "No, because even though I know I didn't have anything to do with her disappearance, someone did. She's not here, she's not at home. I don't know what happened and I fear she might be dead."

Cody blew out a breath. "We'll get our best guys on tracking her down."

"You know how this works. We can't start tracking Keeley until we're put on the case."

"Find some way to get put on the case. Maybe because you're an agent, we'll be forced to investigate."

"Just what the cops want," Noah said. "An FBI agent investigating another FBI agent."

Cody opened his door and stepped out. Noah followed and moved to the group of officers standing beside a cruiser.

"Excuse me, where is Officer Deaver?" Noah asked.

"That's me." A tall man with the beginning of a belly stepped over. "And you are?"

"I'm Noah Grey, we spoke on the phone."

"Oh, yeah." Deaver looked at his notes. "So when did you last see Miss Anderson?"

"Saturday afternoon, around four." Noah's heart sped up.

"What happened?" Cody asked.

"Who is he?" Deaver asked.

"I'm Special Agent Cody Whittaker. I work in organized crime."

"He's a friend," Noah said.

Deaver wrote something in a notebook then looked up at him. "So it looks like you were the last person to have really spent any time with her. Tell me, were you two arguing?"

"No. We spent the day over at the University of Texas San Antonio campus."

"She a student?" Deaver asked.

"No, sir. But she is looking to apply to the art program. We did a tour of the campus, ate lunch, then went back for an art show. She talked to Professor Dunwitty."

"And you weren't having a fight?" Deaver wrote something else then looked up and hit him with a hard stare. "So were you the one banging on her door yesterday?"

He tried not to look guilty. He knew this guy was trying to pin something on him, he just needed to make sure it didn't stick. "I texted Keeley on Sunday, and she didn't answer. Some time after noon, maybe around two or three, I went by her place to see if she was home. She wasn't so I texted her again."

Another cop came over and asked Deaver to follow him. Deaver's gaze shot to Noah and his lips thinned. "Don't leave."

Noah nodded, thinking this was BS. They were wasting time on him. He knew how it went though. He was the primary suspect until they cleared him.

"We've got to get someone on this," Noah whispered to Cody.

"I know, buddy," Cody spoke in low tones too. "If this guy comes back and asks for you to go downtown, we're going to take over the case. They won't like it, but we'll somehow take charge and actually start making progress."

"Good, because I know she's out there."

A few minutes later, Deaver came back, his lips in a deeper frown. "We found a video. It's grainy."

"What did you see?" Noah asked.

"It wasn't you," Deaver admitted then glanced back at the group of officers. "I admit when you called and said you were in law enforcement, I thought, okay, we have our guy. You would know how to do this without getting caught.

The doctor identified one of the men as a guy he hired to fix his busted window. The shot is grainy as fuck, but he was adamant. Plus you don't look like the guy."

"Who did he use to fix the window?" Noah asked.

"Let me look." Deaver flipped through his notebook.

Another car pulled into the lot. Noah turned to see his boss stepping out from her car. He hated that he'd had to call and involve her, but his girlfriend was in trouble, at least he would have support on this in one way or another.

"Some guy named Bill Mendez." Deaver glanced up and snorted. "Doubt the guy's name was Bill."

"Why?" Noah asked.

"Not a Mexican name. I know that may sound racist, but this is San Antonio. You get used to a pattern of names. Bill Mendez doesn't sound right for this area."

Noah said nothing as his boss walked up. "I'm Senior Special Agent Jessica Long. What's going on?"

"Um, yes, ma'am, I'm Officer Deaver. We were called when Doctor Davenport's receptionist showed up. She found the phone, purse, and computer of Kelley Anderson—"

"Keeley," Noah said. "Her name is spelled K E E L E Y."

"Yes, sir. I'll make sure they have that correct." Deaver's made a note of it. "So we came out. When your guy, Agent Grey called and said he was dating Keeley." Deaver's gaze cut to Noah before he continued, "We figured we had our guy, but we weren't positive. Anyway, we found a video, and the doctor identified the person as someone he hired to fix a window."

"So why would he come back to take some woman he doesn't know?" Jessica asked.

"The drugs," Noah said.

"Drugs?" Four people asked at one time.

Noah sighed. No one had mentioned the drugs yet. They'd spent all this time, and they had no clue what they were looking at. "Keeley went to work last Friday and found something under the sink. She thought it was medicines that needed refrigeration because they are packed similar. She cut it open. She had no clue it was cocaine until another person showed up for work. They called the cops and turned it in."

Deaver started looking through his notes, then pulled out his phone and stepped away as he called someone.

"This just put it in our jurisdiction," Jessica said.

"You think they'll fight us on it?" Cody asked. "I mean it's right up my alley. Organized crime and all."

"We can push that angle," Long said. "I think we need to wait for Deaver to come back and tell us what he's found, but Cody, start texting your team and get them on this. We need to be up and rolling within the hour."

"Yes, ma'am. I'll have a mobile command unit sent over. We'll start looking into the men who fixed the window, their known associates, and who could have her. Noah, we'll get our best people on it."

"Thank you, man," Noah said as he shook Cody's hand. "I know you'll do your best."

Cody stepped away. Noah turned back to Jessica. "I should have done more yesterday when she didn't text back and didn't answer my knock at the door."

Jessica shook her head. "How could you have known? How long have you been dating?"

"Not long. We've really only gone out on one real date then we spent Saturday together over by the UT San Antonio campus."

"She a student?" Long asked.

"No ma'am, not yet. Keeley was looking to go back and get her degree in art history then get a masters."

"I'm sorry," Long said. "We'll do everything we can to find her."

Noah could only nod. He had to trust in the process. First forty-eight hours and all that bullshit was true to a point. He knew better than most that she could already be dead. She could be lying in a shallow grave or in a dumpster. The guys who took her wouldn't care what happened to her. She would be like trash, disposable as the napkin they wiped their messy hands with.

Disgust filled him. He had to close his eyes as he clenched his fists. He hated that she'd been abducted, hated that she'd been taken advantage of. This was worse than anything he'd suffered through in his life so far. His heart felt like it was being cut by a million razors while someone poured alcohol on him. He wouldn't survive this. He may not die, but he'd never live again.

CHAPTER TEN

THE ROOM STANK LIKE A BLOCKED-UP GAS STATION bathroom no one ever cleaned. The other woman, Erika, was snoring like she always slept on a hardwood floor with no pillow or blankets. Cold seeped through Keeley. She wanted a pillow, and she needed a shower.

She'd eaten a biscuit. They'd tossed it at her, laughing when it bounced off her head. She'd scrambled for the food, knowing she probably wouldn't get much more. They'd also delivered a water bottle. Only one. But that had saved her.

Light spilled in around the thick curtain on the window across the room. The place was starting to warm, which told her they didn't have central air in this house. The warmth may be a nice change from the cold, but then again, the heat would make the room smell more, though she wasn't sure if it could get any worse.

Erika had been used. The bruised spots in the shape of fingerprints had been visible on her hips and butt when she'd come back into the room. They'd left the lights on for a moment, allowing Keeley to see everything. Before they chained Erika, they'd allowed her to pull on a shirt and underwear. Neither of which covered much. She couldn't imagine walking around naked like Erika had, like it was no big deal to get fucked by strangers and then show her nakedness to everyone.

Keeley shivered. She'd never had rough sex with anyone. All of her partners had been kind so far. Of course, she'd only slept with three guys in her whole life. The first guy had been a mistake. They'd been young and stupid. The second guy she'd fallen in love with, but he'd left her when he decided he needed to find himself. The third guy was special, and they could have had a relationship if he'd stayed in Texas. He'd gotten a job in Florida and asked if she wanted to go with him. She'd thought about it for a few minutes, then realized the last thing in the world she wanted to do was move to Florida. She hadn't ever really loved him, only lusted after him, which would have faded in time.

The door opened, and two guys came in. "Stand up!" The words were yelled. Erika hopped up, and Keeley climbed slowly to her feet. "Time to clean up."

Did that mean a shower? She really hoped that meant a shower. She wanted to scrub off with soap and wash her hair. A toothbrush would be much appreciated too.

"Grab your bucket and come with us. Obey, or we spill that slop all over you."

Keeley held in her whimper as she grabbed the stinky bucket. The chain on her ankle was released, bringing her relief. It didn't last long. She was told to follow. She walked carefully so she didn't spill the mess on her body. They were led into a bathroom and were allowed to pour the bucket into the toilet. It flushed automatically from the weight of the liquid.

"Set the bucket down," one guy said.

She wanted to tell him to go to hell but did as he asked. There would be no easy escape. The men had guns, and she had nothing. She was skilled in the fine art of grabbing tools for a dentist, not combat.

"Tell me, sweetie," one of the guys said as he stroked the side of Erika's face. "Will you suck my dick?"

"No dick sucking," someone said outside the door. It was an older man with a button-down white shirt on. "Get them washed and then get them out here."

"You heard the man," one of the guys said as he started to close the door.

The old man put his hand on the door and pushed it open. "No, open. I want to be able to hear what is going on in here. Strip and wash. That's it. No touching them. They are merchandise."

For a moment, she thought she was close to being saved. The guy wasn't going to let them rape her, but then he said they were merchandise. Her heart squeezed as a whimper escaped. She wasn't going to survive this.

"You heard him. Strip and get clean," one of the jerks who'd come up to get her and Erika snapped.

Erika pulled off the tiny shirt that didn't really cover anything anyways and stood with her breasts out like she didn't care if they saw her. Keeley moved slowly, her hands shaking. These men had guns, and she didn't have a choice. She removed her shirt, and her pants then turned and slid her underwear low before removing her bra. She stepped into the shower with Erika and waited with one arm over her tits, the other hand covering her groin.

Fear and disgust filled her. If she knew how to fight, would she kick and punch her way out or would she be too scared to go against them? This was an impossible situation. These men had guns, and she was trapped. She couldn't get free, and even if she got out of the bathroom, there were more men out there to take her down. What the hell had she gotten herself into? She'd only wanted to be somewhere peaceful to fill out the paperwork for the university, and here she was in some shitty crack house, about to be sold to some asshole.

Erika moved out from under the stream of water and Keeley moved over, washing her body off quickly. She washed her hair then conditioned it while Erika dried. For some reason, Erika didn't seem to mind the men touching her. Keeley couldn't imagine allowing those men to paw at her breasts or run their fingers over her pussy. The sight of them doing that to Erika pissed her off.

After washing and rinsing her body, she drank water straight from the tap. She needed to hydrate. She flipped off the water and reached for the towel. One of the guys grabbed it and held it behind his back. She wasn't going to go after the towel. The asshole could just keep it. She'd drip dry.

The old man stepped to the door; his lips turned down in a frown. "Give her the towel now."

The guy with the towel frowned but handed the scrap of material to her. It wasn't much at all. Instead, it looked like just a tiny piece of thin terrycloth. She longed for her thick bath sheets she'd been given last Christmas by Doc Julian and the towel she used for her hair.

She dried as best as she could then was given a clean dress to slip over her head. Her underwear and bra, as well as her shoes, had been taken. Now all she had was a dress they'd given her. She had been allowed to brush her hair, but not blow it dry or style it.

"Come on, I have things to do," the older man said.

Erika stepped out first, and Keeley followed. They were

led downstairs to the den where four men with guns sat. Keeley was told to stand by the fireplace. Photos were taken of her. She hated everything about this. The man doing the photographs demanded she smile. She didn't. The first punch landed on her ribs. She doubled over and was kicked in the chest.

"Get up and smile, dammit," the guy with the camera roared.

Slowly, she moved to stand, her hands shaking as pain raced through her. She forced a smile, all the while, thinking she would like to kill them.

The old man moved to stand in front of her. "Remove your dress."

She hesitated. The men were all staring at her, lust gleaming in their eyes. There was no way she was going to remove her dress.

The old man grabbed her jaw, squeezing until pain shot down her neck. "Take it off or suffer. Right now, I'm keeping them from fucking you. What do you think they'll do if I let them have you? They will fuck you so hard, use you like you were a doll and you'll bleed for weeks."

The shock made her tingle with fear. Her fingers shook as she tugged up the dress, removing it slowly. The old man ran his fingers over her waist to her breast, cupping it before he tugged on the nipple, squeezing and pulling until she dropped to her knees.

"And that wasn't anything close to what they'll do to you. You want to survive, then do what I ask."

The old guy turned around and stalked over to the chair next to a window. She shivered, fearing what would happen next. The other men were staring at her, their tongues practically hanging out of their mouth.

"Now smile and show us how happy you are. You want a good bid, right?" the guy snapping the photos asked.

A good bid? Like she gave a rat's ass. Who cared how much she was bought for? They were going to eventually kill her. She wouldn't have any life at all. She'd be used and then thrown away when they were done with her. Her hopes, her dreams, they were all gone.

Tears sprang to her eyes, and her nose grew stuffy. The men were animals, pure animals who would hurt her and then hurt her again.

"Put on your dress and stand over here," the old guy said.

Keeley gladly pulled on her dress, hiding her body from the men who looked like they wanted to eat her alive. Photos of Erika were taken, and she didn't seem to mind the attention. Instead, she liked it.

The old man took the camera and began attaching it to a computer. "Now, we wait for a buyer to make a bid."

The door banged open, and everyone turned to look. Two men barged in, dragging someone behind them.

The old man moved around the desk. "What have you got?" His voice boomed throughout the rooms.

The guys dumped the woman on the ground, and Keeley saw she was dressed in a police uniform.

"She was snooping around one of our warehouses," one of the guys said. "So we got her and brought her here."

The old man reached over and slapped the guy on the head. "She's a cop."

"She can be sold like the others."

The cop came to and lunged for the guy next to her. He let his hand fly, slapping her across the face. She didn't stay down, though. Instead, she lunged for him again. This time she reached for his waistband and grabbed a gun.

Keeley watched in horror as the guy grabbed the gun from her and turned it on her. The cop shrunk back, but not before the other guy grabbed her, holding her still.

"Stupid cop," the guy with the gun yelled before he shoved it into her face and pulled the trigger.

Keeley screamed until a hand flew, knocking her to the ground. She fell, whimpering as chaos erupted around her.

"They killed a cop. They killed a cop," Keeley murmured as she tried to get as far away from them as possible. The wall stopped her progress. She was trapped in here with these men and the dead cop.

Keeley started listening. They were saying names now. She'd seen them kill a cop and now she knew the guy's name was Mitchell. She stared at them as they argued. Mitchell was yelling at Amos, the old guy.

"Dad," Mitchell yelled. "She was going for my gun."

"You don't kill cops here!" The old man's face was red, his hands raised as he yelled.

"Calm down, Amos!" another man yelled.

"Don't tell me what to do, Brent." Amos, the old man, stalked over to the computer and stared at the screen. "Well, wouldn't you know it. We have an offer. It took like ten minutes." Amos sat at the computer and frowned. "We could have sold that cop on here. She would have fetched a pretty penny."

Amos hopped up and moved to the cop, toeing her shoulder. Someone had brought in a blanket and was positioning it beside the officer.

"Sorry, Dad, you're right, we could have gotten a lot for her." Mitchell put his arm around Amos's shoulder as they stared down at the dead cop.

Keeley's heart raced, and her head buzzed. She thought she might lose it, but she had to hold herself together. She couldn't afford to freak out. These men were stone-cold killers who happened to be pointing at her.

"Fifty thousand?" Mitchell said.

"Yes, son, you have to stop bringing me women like her." Amos pointed at Erika, who was standing off to the side.

"What's wrong with me?" Erika asked.

"You don't bring in top dollar. The men want this." Amos moved to stand in front of Keeley. He dropped to a squat and reached out, touching her hair. "She is prime meat." The old man turned to look over his shoulder. "Mitchell, this is what we get from here on out. This one fetches us money."

Mitchell's teeth showed in a twisted smile that made Keeley shiver. "Where are we taking her?"

Amos stood and moved to his computer. "Austin. The guy who wants her gave me an address south of Austin. We have a few hours before we have to be there."

Mitchell began undoing his belt buckle as he rubbed his pants. He yanked her up and spun her to face the wall, pressing her against the rough surface. His hands were on her, pinching, tugging. Amos yelled at him then she heard and felt the effects of something hitting Mitchell. The man stepped away, and she dropped to the ground and moved as far away from them as possible. She was near the computer and could see a list of phone numbers. A pen lay on the ground next to her. She picked it up and started writing the numbers on her hand while Mitchell and Amos yelled at each other.

"No sampling the bitches, Mitchell. How many times do I have to tell you?" Amos yelled.

"But she's untested. We need to know what these women have."

She wrote down another number, wishing the names made sense. Instead, it was stuff like Mr. Big City, and Mr. Small Town, OK.

"No, let the buyer break her in," Amos insisted. "That's why he's paying top dollar. He wants to train her himself. We need younger, prettier girls who haven't had sex. I'm sure this one has had sex, but she's pristine. She will be like a virgin for this man."

Mitchell wasn't happy about being told no. His eyes darted to her, and she hid the pen, pretending like she wasn't doing anything. When he looked back at Amos, she wrote down the last of the phone number.

They yelled for another minute before Mitchell threw his hands up in the air. "Fine." Mitchell stepped over to Erika and grabbed her. The woman seemed happy to go to him. Keeley couldn't imagine a world where she would gladly be passed from guy to guy.

"Get the bitch cleaned up. The buyer wants her tonight," Amos said.

Two guys came at Keeley, their lips set in grimaces, their anger evident. Did they want to screw her too? Amos didn't seem to be backing down. He wasn't going to allow anyone to touch her.

They shoved her into a chair and brought over a wet cloth, washing her face. One guy brushed her hair, tugging the tangled strands hard. She wanted to tell him to go to hell, but the last thing she needed was them figuring out a way to punish her.

"I need to pee," Keeley said, praying she could escape through the bathroom.

Amos turned to stare at her. "Take her to the bathroom, Diego."

"Fuck. Are you serious?" the guy who'd brushed her hair asked.

Amos lifted his hand like he would hit Diego. "Yes, now get to it."

She had a plan, it was terrible, but maybe it would work. Diego led her to the bathroom. She expected the door to close, but he didn't move away. Instead, he watched her.

"Go on, then." Diego waved his hand. "Do your business then let's get back into the other room."

"I can't pee with you standing there."

"Tough shit. I'm not moving. Pee or let's go back in."

Keeley pulled up her dress, trying to hide as much of her body as she could from the man and sat on the toilet. He never stopped watching, which grossed her out. How could these guys do this? Didn't they have any humanity left in them?

She finished, then washed her hands. She didn't have a way to escape. Diego took her back into the main room where Mitchell was having sex with Erika. The other guys were watching, lust filling their gazes. Keeley had never felt so in danger in her life. There was no escape. She was trapped.

CHAPTER ELEVEN

NOAH SAT BENT FORWARD, HIS HEAD RESTING ON HIS arms. It had been a long night with little sleep. They were no closer to finding Keeley or the men who had taken her. Tears had come, fear for her had exploded, but they still didn't have her. She was lost to him, never to be seen again.

The door opened, and he sat up, seeing his boss step into the room.

"How are you holding up?" Long asked.

He ran his hand through his hair, the frustration threatening to spill out. Yelling at Long wouldn't do any good. He settled for defeat. "I'm not."

"You do look like you've been run through the wringer. Maybe go home and get some rest."

He shook his head. "I can't leave, not yet."

"You aren't doing yourself any favors, not resting. I know it's hard—"

"How do you know it's hard?" He was a dick for asking her that question.

"Okay, you got me on that." Long set a cup of coffee

down in front of him. "I don't know what it feels like to have your girlfriend abducted. I know she must be terrified. I would be."

"She's not trained like we are." A growl escaped his lips as he fought to contain the anger. "She's young too. She has so much of her life in front of her."

Long sat next to him and pulled out her tablet, opening it to the case reports they had on Keeley's abduction. He stared at what they had so far, the words mixing as his eyes blurred.

He took a swig of coffee then set the cup down before leaning back in the chair and growled in frustration. He stared up at the ceiling, trying to figure out how he could help her. His brain hurt.

There were no answers or at least no right answers. She'd been abducted by a group of organized criminals who knew how to hide. His job, stopping drugs, along with Cody's job of eliminating organized crime was supposed to prevent this kind of crap, but they weren't close to ending organized crime or stopping the drugs that kept the crime organizations in business. They were failures.

"We'll figure it out," Long said.

The door opened, and Cody stepped in. "Still nothing. I'm searching everywhere I know to look. We've raided four places, and still, we've got nothing."

Noah nodded and flicked through more of the files on Long's tablet. The words bled together, and he wanted to say something, but he had problems coming up with anything. "She can't just...maybe there some way we have... Jesus, she can't just disappear into thin air. Just like those guys couldn't be gone. They're out there somewhere."

"We've got our best teams on it," Long said.

"I need to shower." Noah stood, ache radiating down his back to his knees. He felt old as pain filled his head. He stumbled to the door. "I'll be back this afternoon."

"You okay driving?" Cody asked.

He drew in a slow breath and blew it out before nodding. "I'm good."

"Get some rest," Long said before he shut the door.

Leaving the FBI offices was nearly impossible. There was a part of him that felt that if he stayed, maybe he could find her. But him being at the FBI building wasn't changing anything. Like Long said, they had the best people on it. He'd been going hard at it for hours. Now he was hardly able to see enough to drive home. His mind kept blanking, and the anger was close to winning, leaving him wanting to rip into people instead of helping them solve this case.

He set his alarm for three hours and stretched out, falling asleep before his head hit the pillow. The beeping from his phone jolted him awake. At first, he couldn't remember what city he lived in or what he'd been doing. Then reality rolled in, crushing his heart. He had to find Keeley.

He took a cold shower and stopped by a sandwich place for food. At the FBI offices, he found they'd made little progress. They had arrested fifteen people, but none of them were connected to Keeley's disappearance.

Even with all of the resources he had at the FBI, they couldn't find Keeley. It was a wonder they ever found anyone.

He spent hours looking. Depression seeped in, filling him with misery. It was almost seven in the evening on Tuesday, and Keeley had been gone for way too long. If another night passed and they still hadn't found her, he knew what that would mean. Statistics didn't lie. Somewhere, someone was doing evil, and he had no way to stop them.

Tears burned the back of his eyes, but he pushed them away. He couldn't fall apart yet. The door opened, and Cody stepped in.

"I'm headed out. I need a few hours' sleep."

Noah swallowed over the emotions. He appreciated how much Cody had helped him. "Gottcha," he said.

"Amber knows to wake me if anyone calls. She'll make sure I'm up and back here in minutes."

Noah nodded as he stared at the file one more time. "It's like they all disappeared."

"Sucks. I feel like we're close to something."

Noah stared at the file, feeling like he should say something, but he didn't know what he could possibly add to the conversation. They'd been working since Monday morning. He'd gone home for a nap, the rest of the guys needed sleep too. Maybe he shouldn't have left to sleep for three hours, but those three hours had allowed him to sit in this conference room and comb through files, searching for clues. His brain had been frazzled before, now he could focus. They hadn't found exactly who they were looking for, but they had put pieces together to take down other organized crime groups.

Most of the office headed home for a few hours' sleep. He stayed and kept looking. The men who'd fixed Doc Julian's window had given false information. They were untraceable. Their phone had been tossed, and their business address was fake. They didn't have good enough photos for facial recognition software to do much other than make a guess. Overall, it was a bust.

It was getting dark, and a storm was moving in. Noah closed his eyes to rest them for a moment. Someone had ordered in sandwiches, and he needed to grab one, but first, he needed a moment to think. It seemed like he was close, but that might have only been hopes and wishes making him believe they had a chance of finding Keeley.

CHAPTER TWELVE

She'd been given water. That was it. No food, just water. She would kill for a slice of pizza, maybe not kill, but hunger gnawed at her like rats on wood.

Thunder crashed outside, and she flinched. How long had she been here? The hours and minutes slipped away. Erika had been used multiple times and was lying in a heap on the floor.

The door cracked open, the light blinding her. "Time to go," Amos said.

She recoiled, wishing she could just have some water before they took her wherever they were going. After washing her face and combing her hair, they'd stuck her back in the room upstairs, tossing Erika in with her before coming back to grab her twice more. The poor woman looked like a ragdoll tossed on the ground.

Mitchell grabbed Keeley's arm and squeezed hard. Pain filled her, and she cried out. He punched her in the ribs, making her drop to the ground.

"Get up, bitch."

She struggled to standing. The man shoved her up

against the wall, his breath hot on her neck. She tried to get away, but he held her still. His hand came down on her breast and squeezed hard, leaving her gasping.

"You like that, don't you? You'd love it if I shoved in and fucked your ass, wouldn't you? I bet you'd take it dry and love every second of me filling your ass with my thick cock."

Tears ran down her face as she struggled against his hold. His tongue came out and licked up her cheek. Her shivers couldn't be contained. He lifted his knee and pushed his leg against her center, grinding hard.

A door across from them opened. Keeley stared inside, hardly believing what she saw. Kids. More than four kids were in that room. They watched, unblinking as Mitchell punched her again before he grabbed her nipple and pulled so hard she cried out.

"If Amos had left, I'd fuck you until you bled."

What was with these men and making women bleed. Mitchell glanced over his shoulder and chuckled. "Maybe I should make you watch me fuck one of those kids. I bet you'd be on your knees begging me to take you after that."

Keeley wanted to throw up. She shoved him hard, struggling with him.

"Yeah, keep at it. I like it when they struggle. Makes it more satisfying."

Bile rose in her throat. She wanted to kill the man.

"Mitchell, get down here," Amos called up the stairs.

"Fuck." Mitchell cursed before he punched her in the gut.

She doubled over, coughing and gagging. Mitchell didn't give her time to recover. He tugged her down the stairs and dragged her out to the car, his grip punishing. He used zip strips to hold her hands in front of her body and then strapped her in the center seat. Before he moved away, he kissed her, trying to force her mouth open, but she held her lips closed. After a moment, he pulled back then spit in her face. The door was slammed, and Mitchel walked away. She was shocked the man didn't get in the car with her.

The driver was a stranger to her as well as the man in the passenger seat. If Mitchell had come, she would have probably been raped before she arrived at the final destination. Who knew what these two would do?

The rain came down hard. Keeley hated driving in weather like this, but she didn't want to be back in that house. Somehow she would get away. She had to.

The driver cranked the engine and took off. Lightning flashed, and thunder boomed. She screamed. The two men in the front seat laughed. Her nerves were on edge. How could she survive if thunder and lightning scared her? She would never make it to freedom. She stuffed the sob threatening to erupt. She would never be free again. Her life was over. Whoever had bought her would make sure she never lived another moment for herself.

The car sped up. They'd been in San Antonio the whole time. She knew the area and which turns they were making. She tried to keep track of every road, every freeway, so if she ever got away, she could tell someone where the house was.

The rain got worse, and the traffic slowed. "Goddammit," the driver yelled as they slowed to a stop. Traffic was being directed to the off ramp, and they were driving on the surface streets. The car turned down a side road, sliding a little on the wet pavement.

"Fuck, be careful," the man in the passenger seat said.

"Shut up, Denver. I'm fine." The driver didn't slow. Instead, he sped up.

The roads were slick and the rain torrential. The population thinned out as the road twisted and turned. She had no clue where they were. They turned then turned again, passing a gas station along the way. There were a few houses she guessed, or at least a few places out in the dark fields with their lights on.

"Think we could pull over and sample the bitch?" The rough words from the driver made her want to vomit. He reached back and grabbed her hair, tugging her forward. "We could fuck her mouth. No one would know."

She gagged and tried to pull away. The driver lifted up off his ass and slapped her. She fell to the side and closed her eyes, wishing this was all a nightmare.

"Watch out," Denver yelled.

The car started to fishtail as they entered a curve. She couldn't brace herself because she was cuffed and reaching to the side would make her twist too much.

"I'm fine," the driver snapped.

But they weren't. The car was over the line, and they hadn't slowed. There was another curve up ahead. She didn't think he could correct. Everything was wrong with the situation, and the asshole was speeding up.

They rounded the next curve too fast. Their car lights splashed on something in the road. She screamed as they smashed into the object. The harsh scrape of metal on metal filled the car.

They started to spin, first left then right. The back of the car dipped. They'd hit the ditch. Her shoulder belt locked down and she was held in place as the car flipped. Something flew through the air, hitting her in the face. Pain flashed, taking her breath.

She may have still been screaming, she wasn't sure. One of the doors popped open and was ripped off before they finally settled half on the road, half off.

Rain still came down, and lightning flashed. Both men in the front weren't moving. Were they dead? She didn't have time to check.

Her hands were still bound together, but she twisted, sending pain up her arm. This was life or death, and she couldn't worry about a little pain. She could fix her arm later.

She twisted more as she fought the button on the seat buckle. Pain hit hard, going from her shoulder up her neck to her head. She almost screamed, but she bit down on her lips, staying quiet. If the men in the front were alive, the last thing she wanted was to have them notice what she was doing.

Finally, the buckle popped, and she was free.

She slid over, ignoring the pain in her head and neck though it stole her breath as she scrambled to get out of the car. The open door, the one that had been ripped off, was positioned right over a drainage ditch. She didn't have any options. It was this way or die.

Keeley stepped out and almost fell when her feet dropped far. Her knees were in water, and the only thing that kept her from toppling over was a branch of a tree she was forced to grab. Pain sliced through her hand.

"Mother of God!" It was a mesquite tree with thorns more than an inch long.

Keeley couldn't help but cry out though she was trying hard to stay quiet. She really didn't want the men in the front to wake up. She pulled her hand off the tree, causing more pain as the thorn went back through the hole. There was little light, but she could tell something dark was running down her arm.

Tears threatened, but she couldn't give up. She had to fight.

Getting to the street in the slippery mud took almost a minute. Her head spun, and dizziness prevailed. Giving up would be so easy. Fear filled her and made her press on. Which way had they come from? There were few houses, only the road, trees—too bad they had thorns—and fields. She closed her eyes, forcing herself to think.

She prayed she picked the right way as she headed out.

Keeley ran. She ran for her life, for safety, for freedom. After what seemed way too long to be such a short distance, she passed the thing they'd hit. It looked to be metal siding of some sort like maybe the roof had blown off a barn or something, or perhaps junk had fallen off the back of a truck. She didn't stop. Instead, she ran past the heap of metal and around the curve.

No car lights flashed in the distance. She was alone. The rain came down harder, blowing in sheets, slashing across her face.

She ran.

They'd taken her shoes. Tiny pebbles on the road felt like knives in her feet.

She ran.

Lightning struck nearby, and she swore the hair on her neck sizzled as it rose, but she couldn't stop. If they caught up, she'd never see the light of day again. They were being paid fifty-thousand dollars for her. She didn't even make that much in a year.

She ran.

Again the sky filled with light as lightning flashed across the cloud bank. Keeley swore she saw the beginnings of a tornado dropping low. She didn't have time to worry about tornados or rain, her life was on the line.

She ran.

Up ahead, she saw a light. Her heart sped up. She

choked on the water that had run down her face and into her mouth. Maybe she'd find a savior in all this mess. Over choking coughs, she prayed for help, begging God to save her.

Stumbling toward the light, she kept those prayers up. Her feet ached, and pain laced up her calves to her knees. Her hand hurt, and dizziness made walking hard and running almost impossible. Breathing took effort, but she would make it to that light even if hell opened the ground and the devil reached up for her, she would make it to that freaking light.

It was closer. She could make out a gravel parking lot. Rocks ground into her heels, but she didn't slow as she raced around to the front of the building. There were no lights on. Her throat closed as tears ran down her face. She banged on the door, screaming into the storm.

Depression twisted deep. No one was at this little store. Her legs gave out as she slumped against the door, wondering how she would survive the night.

Before, when she'd been running, trying to escape, she hadn't noticed the cold, but here, under the awning of the gas station and the harsh blinking florescent lights, the wind blew in, chilling her to the bone.

Tears flowed, and sobs wracked her body. She coughed as snot ran down her face. She was a mess, but she was still alive.

Car lights bounced across the pavement. She struggled to standing, praying the person didn't pass her by. Who would stop for her? Not someone like herself. She might call the cops, but no way would she stop for some shoeless, wet rag of a woman, dripping snot and spittle while looking homeless or worse — looking like a crack whore most likely.

The lights splashed across the lot and hit her. She lifted

her hands, blinking against the brightness as pain filled her. She'd forgotten about her arm.

"Wait," she called out, but her voice was small against the raging rain and the booming thunder.

The car drove past and hope faded. Then it stopped and backed up. She blinked against the drops in her eyes, struggling to see through the dizziness that hazed her vision. Was that a cop?

Her heart sped up. Could she really be rescued?

The car stopped and she stumbled over. Was this real? More tears blurred her vision. She heard the engine noise but thought she was making it up. She doubted the car was really here until her hands landed on the metal. She cried out as relief filled her.

She was rescued.

All the hope Keeley had of being saved had felt unreal until this moment. She would make it home. Her breath came in gasps.

Maybe, just maybe she really would get her degree in art history. The thought almost brought her to her knees as she moved closer to the police car.

The ping off the back of the car made her stop. She looked over and saw the man who had been in the passenger seat, Denver, standing at the road. He fired again, missing and hitting the car.

Tears filled Keeley's eyes as she stumbled to the front of the car and ducked, toppling to the ground. The cop's door banged open. More gunfire erupted; this time closer. She screamed again.

The cop had parked where the front of the car wasn't under the awning so rain pelted her. She didn't care, all she wanted was for Denver to die.

She sucked in a harsh breath. Never in her life had she wished someone dead, but the asshole had taken too much.

Keeley had her arms over her head as she curled into a ball, praying the cop killed Denver. The shooting stopped. She saw a black shoe in front of her. The shoe touched her foot, and she flinched before she uncovered her head and looked up. It was the cop.

He met her gaze and glanced at her still cuffed hands. His lips turned down in a deeper frown. "Just a moment ma'am. Say here. Don't move. I've called for backup and an ambulance. I'm going to make sure he's down."

"Kill him," Keeley choked out.

Guilt filled her for saying it out loud until the cop's lips twitched into a smile. She prayed they could find the rest of the gang based on Denver and the other guy in the car. She had a feeling the guy's name wasn't Denver though.

The whine of sirens grew closer. Tears flowed freely. She was going to make it. Her hand had been punctured, and blood still flowed, her feet were cut, and she was freezing, she'd been hit and was bruised, but she would live.

Another cop car pulled up and then an ambulance parked under the protection of the cover above. She let the tears flow, not caring that snot and probably blood was on her face.

"Hey there, hon," a female voice said above her. "I'm going to take those cuffs off you."

A woman, a little older than her, knelt in front of her. Purple gloves covered the woman's hands. The cuffs were removed and placed in an envelope.

Keeley guessed that was for evidence. She hoped they got something off the cuffs. She hadn't fought back when she'd been placed in the car or when she'd been hit, so she didn't have their skin under her nails. She'd watched too many cops shows for there not to be evidence under her fingernails. In the moment, she hadn't even thought of reaching out and touching any of those men.

"My name is Mindy, I'm a paramedic with the South Hays Fire District. We're just south of San Marcos. We're probably going to take you over to Resolute. The ambulances from that wreck on the freeway that has the traffic snarled are all going to Central Texas Hospital."

Keeley nodded, not knowing what to say. Did she need a hospital? She wasn't that bad. She was about to tell the woman she was fine and could walk home, but there was something wrong with what the lady had said.

"Wh-where are we?"

"Just south of San Marcos, near the outlets."

Another man came over with the stretcher, he had on purple gloves too. He knelt next to Mindy.

"I'm Chad, I'm an EMT, I'll be driving your chariot tonight. I'm a professional driver in my spare time, so don't worry." He winked and shot her a huge smile. "I'll get you there safe and sound." Chad turned to Mindy. "Do you need anything?"

"We're going to start an IV when we get in the bus. I don't know that we need any meds. Can you help me get her on the stretcher?"

"I can stand," Keeley said.

"I'm sure you can." Chad looped his hand under her arm. "We're just going to provide an assist. Watch much basketball?"

Keeley shook her head, which might have been a mistake because the dizziness returned. "No, not really."

"That's okay. I don't either."

"What's your name?" Mindy asked once she was settled on the stretcher.

Chad started strapping her to the device, and she jerked at the straps. He glanced up and shot her another smile. "This is just for safety. I won't make them tight, and once we get to the hospital and aren't driving, they will be removed."

She settled then looked at Mindy. "My name is Keeley Anderson."

"Okay Keeley, it looks like you're ready to transport."

The cop came over and Keeley gasped. How could she have forgotten about Erika and the rest of the kids?

She reached for the cop, her fingers twisting on his arm. "They have them."

The cop lifted his eyebrows. "What?"

"They have more. They were in the house. Kids. They are selling them. You have to call Noah."

"Slow down," the cop said. "Who is Noah?"

"He's with the FBI in San Antonio. I don't have my phone, and I don't remember his number, but I have these." She opened her palm and held up her hand. "Take a photo, they are starting to wear off."

"What is that?" Mindy asked.

"The numbers of people wanting to buy humans," Keeley said.

Mindy, Chad, and the two cops stared at her, speechless. She drew in a shaky breath.

"They were taking me to Austin. A guy bought me for —" Bile rose in her throat, and she sputtered as she coughed.

The cop used his shoulder mic and started talking. "I need to get a message to Noah—what's his last name, miss?"

"Grey," she said.

"I need to get a message to Noah Grey of the FBI based in San Antonio. There is a woman here, who is talking about human trafficking." The cop stopped talking and waited as words were said over his radio. "Yes, Noah Grey of the FBI in San Antonio."

"We're loading her up. Follow us to Resolute," Mindy said.

The stretcher was pushed into the back of the ambulance. Mindy crawled up with her and began working. An IV was set up and Mindy pushed the needle in before the ambulance started moving.

"Okay, I have to ask, were you sexually assaulted?"

Keeley shook her head. "No. Thank God they wanted to sell me to someone who wanted a pristine woman, not someone heavily used. It was the only thing that saved me."

She shivered as she thought of the kids. The nightmare they would go through. She hated the idea of them being used like trash. Noah needed to get the information about the house and where those girls were being kept. She feared what would happen to them otherwise, and she feared what would happen to herself when the bastards found out she hadn't been delivered. Would they come for her?

CHAPTER THIRTEEN

Noah's phone rang, and he sat up, groaning as his body rebelled against the movement. He'd been in this chair too damn long. He stood as he answered, stretching his back as he lifted his free arm over his head.

"Special Agent Noah Grey, what can I do for you."

"I have a San Marcos police officer on the line. He said he found Keeley Anderson."

"What?" Noah's heart jackrabbited to racing. He reached out and grabbed the table, holding on with his free hand. "Put him through."

The line clicked twice before he heard someone speaking.

"Hello, this is Special Agent Noah Grey."

"Agent Grey, do you know a Keeley Anderson?"

"Yes." His heart nearly exploded.

"She said to call you and tell you about a house with kids in it and human trafficking. I'm Officer Del Bishop up here in San Marcos."

"Is she okay?" Noah knew he should care about the

other stuff, but he needed to know if Keeley was going to live.

The door opened, and his boss stepped in. He waved Long over, grabbing her arm when she was close enough. He put the phone on speaker while the officer was talking.

"Going to be fine. She's been beaten up, bloody and bruised, she's probably suffering from hypothermia, but she's in the ambulance headed to Resolute outside of New Braunfels."

"What did she say? This is Senior Special Agent Jessica Long."

"She said something about human trafficking, girls, and being sold to someone in Austin. Honestly, it didn't make much sense, but I know there is an uptick in trafficking in the area. You guys gave a presentation a few weeks ago. Agent Cody Whittaker, I believe."

"Yes, I'm glad his work is helping. Thank you for calling," Long said. "We'll send an agent out to Resolute."

"There's a wreck up here, shut down the interstate. Let me send an officer over and be with her while we finish up here. The guy who I guess had her, well he's dead now. I had to shoot him."

"There's a guy?"

"Sure is. He's big, looks mean."

"Does he have any ID?" Noah asked.

"Let me see."

He could hear someone talking and something making noise, rain maybe. He moved to his laptop and pulled up the weather. Sure enough, near San Marcos, the rain was coming down hard. Long texted Cody and told him that Agent Whittaker was on his way in.

"Yeah, you all still there?" the cop asked.

"Yes, both Agent Long and Grey are here," Long said.

"Okay, so he has no ID. He has money in his wallet, but nothing to identify him. We've got a mess from the wreck up here, but as soon as we have some officers free, we'll go looking for the car this guy was in. I've sent another officer to the hospital to talk to Miss Anderson. If you give me your number, I'll text it to him and have him call you as soon as he gets into the room with her."

"Sure." Noah rattled off his number and waited for the officer to say he'd received it.

"Got it."

"Thank you, Officer Bishop. We'll have someone on their way to meet you," Long said. "With traffic the way it looks, it will take a while, but we'll be out there as soon as we can. And unfortunately, with the weather so bad, we'll have to drive."

"Yes, ma'am. I'll be here. It looks like clearing this scene isn't taking priority. I've covered the body with a tarp, but honestly, there's so much rain evidence will probably wash away."

"How bad is the wreck up there?" Noah asked.

"Fifteen cars and four eighteen-wheelers along with a cattle transport truck. It's going to take the better part of the night. They're sending in help from Austin, but we just don't have enough resources to get through all the cars."

"Wow, that's bad," Noah said.

"Yes, sir. I'm going to let you go and see if I can find anyone else to help me look around out here. The rain is finally letting up."

"We'll be in touch," Long said before she pushed the button to end the call.

The door opened, and Cody stepped in. "Ma'am, you texted?"

"Thank you for coming in, Agent Whittaker, we found Keeley Anderson."

Cody's gaze swung to Noah. "Alive?"

"Yes, she's talking too." Noah's phone dinged, and he scooped it up, staring at a photo that had come through.

"What's that?" Cody asked.

"I don't—" Another text came through from Officer Bishop. "He says Keeley had written down the numbers from a computer. They are people who want to buy humans. She said she'd been sold to someone in Austin."

"Shit," Cody said. "We've got to find out more. I need to know where this house is, who the people are." Cody turned to Long. "Who is going to see Keeley?"

"Well, I figured Agent Grey would probably go because I didn't think I could stop him. You should drive up too, take a few agents. We need someone to meet with the officer at the scene where they found Keeley."

"I'll round up some people," Cody said.

Noah stared at the map. The direct path to Austin was red, indicating heavy traffic. "We should take I10."

"Got it," Cody said. "I'll see you out there." Cody turned to leave but came back and pulled him into a hug. "We'll get these bastards."

Noah choked down the sob threatening to spill out. Relief filled him. He was overwhelmed. Keeley had been found.

"Noah," Long said. "Be careful. I'll call you later. I'm staying here to assemble a tactical team for when we enter the house where she was held."

"We don't know where that was."

Long lifted her brows. "Yet. I'll have someone go to the hospital who can recreate where she was based on what she remembers. We'll figure it out."

"Thank you," Noah said. "And thank you for being so patient."

"While you're there, get as much information as you can from her. I know you care for her, but the more we know, the faster we can shut them down."

"Yes, ma'am. I'll see what we can do. I want them in jail for taking her."

"I know, and we're going to figure it out." Long grabbed his shoulder and squeezed. "Go, be with her."

He nodded as he gathered his laptop and his phone. He had a change of clothes in the car along with a travel pack of necessities in his bag. He would be fine.

The drive to the hospital took a little over an hour. It looked like I35 was still clogged. When he'd lived in New York, he and a few friends had driven to upstate during the winter and run into a traffic-stalling storm that caused all kinds of havoc. They'd pulled into the lot of a restaurant and were about to go in when a sixty-five car pileup clogged the interstate. It had taken the cops a full day to clear the roadway. He and his friends decided to get a bottle of tequila, some beer, and a pizza then they checked into a hotel. They'd spent the next forty-eight hours eating pizza, playing cards, and watching porn. The roads cleared and they were sober so they headed home and he never drove to the upper part of the state in the winter. He didn't envy the guys working this wreck. There was one lane moving, but that was it.

Noah headed inside and checked in at the front desk. The woman told him how to get back to the ER where he was allowed in to see Keeley.

Her eyes were closed, and she appeared to be asleep. She had cuts on her face, her hands were bandaged. Her hair was a mess and bruises darkened her cheeks like someone had hit her. Anger rose.

He swallowed over the pain and moved closer. This woman was meant to be his, no question. His heart squeezed as he stared down at her beautiful face. He hated the bruises, but he loved seeing her. There was no way he was going to let her get away. He knew long-term relationships weren't perfect, but he didn't want perfect, he wanted someone to argue with, someone to care for, someone to keep him on his toes, and make him better.

She blinked open her eyes, confusion filling her gaze for a moment then her lips spread into a broad smile.

"You're here." Her voice was scratchy and thick with emotions.

His throat closed and he had to swallow before he could talk. "I couldn't stay away. You're safe. My God, I've been so worried about you."

She tried to sit up, but he placed his hand on her shoulder. She blew out an exasperated breath. "I want to go home."

"I'm sure you do, but I need information. I need to know everything you know."

She sucked in air through her nose, blowing out in a huff. He watched her features change as she concentrated. Pride filled him. She wasn't falling apart, instead she was rallying.

"Okay," she said. "It's a lot. Did you get the phone numbers?"

"Yes, they were texted to the FBI. Right now there is a team searching out those numbers, looking for the people behind them."

"Austin," she glanced up, her eyes wide. "Were you

able to get someone to Austin to find out who was going to buy me?"

His muscles clenched as he thought of some slimy asshole buying Keeley. He wanted to rip the person apart, but he had to stay calm and focus on the task at hand.

"No, we don't even know where to look."

She shrugged. "I don't know exactly where they were taking me. I know where the house I was held in is."

Hope rose. "You do?"

"Yes. Can I get a map? Like a real one, something printed so I can draw on it?"

"Give me a few minutes, and I'll see what I can do."

"South of Fredericksburg and I10 and west of it too."

"Awesome. I'll print that out."

He bent over her and kissed her forehead so gently he wondered if she felt his lips, but then she sighed and relaxed. He stared into her eyes, hoping he communicated how much he cared for her before heading out of the room.

It took him a few minutes to convince the duty nurse to allow him to print a map. After success, he headed to her room with five printed pages in hand. Keeley had lifted the head of her bed and had the table close by. He set the pages down in front of her.

"I need a pen," she said.

"Sure thing." He grabbed one from his bag and handed it to her.

Keeley found the map she wanted and stared at it. She chewed on her fingernail for a moment before picking up the pen.

"When I was a kid, my dad used to have me trace my route on a map. He never wanted me to get lost. It's one of the good memories I have of him. Anyway, I know I was at

Fredericksburg and I10. We'd driven over the train tracks twice before we got onto the freeway, and we'd made a sharp left turn after passing under the bridge. That meant we were on Cincinnati street."

Noah followed her progress on his iPad, excited they had a very good idea where the house was located.

"We drove about three blocks after making a right turn. The house was on — on the right because we made a left out of an alleyway. We came out of the yard, they were parked in a fenced in back yard, and they drove out, turning right into the alley, then left on the street. We went down a few blocks and made a right. We crossed over a little creek and under the freeway. Then we turned left and drove before making a right onto the interstate. They took the 410 and then we took I35. I didn't realize we were in the car that long. I might have drifted off. I was tired and it was raining. They found me in San Marcos."

Noah drilled in on the area Keeley had described, pulling up the picture of a house next to an alley on Calaveras St. Her eyes narrowed as she stared at the photo on the iPad.

"That's what it looked like," Keeley said. "I'm very sure that's it."

"How sure?" He held his breath as she met his gaze.

"Close to one hundred percent."

"Wow, you're amazing. I need to call my boss and send her this address. Anything else you remember, write it down. You're amazing with details. Thank you so much."

He took a screenshot of the house then backed out on the map and took a screenshot of the streets. He sent both photos to his boss along with the address, stating that Keeley was ninety-nine percent sure. After he sent the text with the address, his phone rang. It was Long.

"Are you sure?" Long's voice sounded strained.

"Let her tell you what she told me." He turned to Keeley. "This is Senior Special Agent in Charge Jessica Long on the phone, she's my boss. Could you tell her what you told me about how you know where the address is?"

"Um, sure." Keeley sat up straighter and cleared her throat. "Okay so I know we got onto I10 at Fredericksburg. My dad taught me how to navigate and remember where I was going at all times, so I didn't get lost. This was important, so I paid attention to this part. We turned right on the frontage road at I10 and crossed over train tracks. We'd turned left to get onto Fredericksburg which means we were on Cincinnati. Before that, we'd driven three blocks and had crossed over the train tracks and under the freeway. We'd also crossed a small stream. To get onto Cincinnati, we'd turned right. We'd driven out of a backyard, turning right into an alley, then left onto the street. Noah showed me a shot of the front of the house, that's what it looked like."

"Dear Lord," Long said. "If only everyone else had your ability to keep track of where you were."

"It was raining, and I think I fell asleep on the freeway. We were on 410 and then I35 until the wreck. The rain was really coming down, and the lighting was bad where they exited the freeway."

"They found the car," Long said. "So we know where that was. It was empty by the way."

"Oh, the names Amos, that's the dad and Mitchell, that's the son. Also, a Brent was there, and Denver was the name of the guy who chased me to the gas station. The cop killed him."

"Thank you, Keeley," Long said. "This really helps.

Anything else you can tell Agent Grey, we'd appreciate it. Any detail, no matter how small."

"There were children in those rooms. I was put up for sale. Those kids, he's going to sell them too. He's been doing it for a while. They have a network of buyers."

"We're working on those numbers you gave us," Long said. "We'll find them and shut them down."

He picked up the phone and clicked the button to stop using the speaker. "I'm on with you now. Anything specific for me?"

"Just keep doing what you're doing. Keeley is giving great information. We might catch the bastards yet."

"Keep me updated," he said.

"Sure thing, and spend some time with Keeley, you deserve some downtime."

"Thank you."

He hung up and moved to stand next to the bed. "I'm so thankful you survived."

"I'm thankful they didn't rape me."

"Me too, but honestly, I would still feel the same about you."

She looked up at him, studying his face. "How's that?"

"I realized a few things. I can't waste time. You're precious. I don't want to wait to tell you that I'm falling for you. Maybe if this hadn't happened, I might have told you in a few months."

She lifted her eyebrows as she stared at him. "What does that mean to you?"

"It means that my heart can't live without you. I want you in my life. I know you're going through some stuff with wanting to change careers, and you'll be busy with school. I'm busy with my job too, but I think if we both understand each other, and not put restraints on when we can see each other, we can make this work."

He couldn't believe he was bringing this up now, but he needed her to know how he felt. If she turned him down it would hurt. He almost blurted out the question he wanted to ask, but he held back as doubts surfaced. If she left him, there was no way he would survive.

CHAPTER FOURTEEN

NOAH LIFTED HIS HAND AND CHEWED HIS NAIL AS HIS stomach squeezed. Keeley was quiet for a moment then her eyebrows lifted. "Restraints?"

"If you're in school until late, and I'm working, if we aren't willing to see each other like at midnight and go to sleep together, we'd never see each other."

Her lips pressed together, and her eyes went unfocused for a moment before she met his gaze again. "Are you asking me to move in?"

"I don't know. It sounds crazy, I know, but I want you to think about maybe we shouldn't measure our relationship by what is usual or what other people think we should do. I just don't want to blow this with you because we're both too busy to see each other and then we don't communicate."

Keeley nodded and closed her eyes. Worry filled him then Keeley reached for his hand and squeezed.

"I like the idea of being open to possibilities like maybe spending more time together than we would have in a traditionally-paced relationship. I'm not saying I want to move in, but honestly, I'm a little afraid of being alone right now."

He bent and kissed her forehead. "I'm here for you."

She opened her eyes, and his breath stalled. This woman seemed to stare right into his soul. He wished they were really alone, and he could pull her into his arms and make a connection even time wouldn't break.

"What are you thinking about?" Keeley asked.

"You."

Her eyes narrowed. "What about me?"

"How you see into me. It's like you're looking into my soul."

"The look in your eyes was so intense."

"I feel very intense about you. I can't explain it. There's a connection I've never felt before. It's like we are supposed to be together."

She sighed and closed her eyes again. The door opened, and a guy in a button-down shirt and tie stepped in.

"Hello Miss Anderson, I'm Doctor Terrell. I was called when you came in. I usually don't work the ER, but when cases like yours happen, they call me. I would have been here earlier, but traffic was snarled."

"Cases like mine?" Keeley looked from Noah to the doctor.

"Yes. I work with trafficked victims. I know it seems like a small field, but the number of women and men in the area is rather large. I specialized in gynecology then went back and worked on psychology, and that's more why I'm here. I don't expect you to want to answer any questions or have any for me right now, but I have an office here in New Braunfels and one in San Antonio."

Noah had been standing off to the side, but he stepped up and reached out to shake the doctor's hand. "I'm Special Agent Noah Grey from the FBI. I'm in San Antonio. Are you in contact with anyone from our office?"

Doctor Terrell grasped his hand and shook. "No, I'm not at the moment. I do work with a few detectives on San Antonio's police force, but we haven't involved the FBI. We figured this wasn't something you all would be interested in."

"We're interested," Noah said. "I'd like to talk to you once we're out of here."

"Are you here for professional reasons?" Terrell asked. "I wasn't aware the FBI jumped in so early on cases."

"Yes and no."

"We're dating," Keeley interjected.

Noah reached out and took her hand. "We are dating. As soon as we learned she was abducted, the FBI stepped in to help. I'm coordinating with the FBI office. We've narrowed the location where we believe the house she was held is. I haven't heard back from my boss. Hopefully, they'll find the bastard who is running the operation and rescue some people."

"There were a lot of kids in the house," Keeley said.

Doctor Terrell looked shocked. "Kids?"

"Yes. I was locked in a room with another woman. There were three rooms I passed by, and one of the doors was open. I glanced in and saw at least five, maybe eight kids chained to the floor."

Doctor Terrell shook his head. "Damn, that's worse than I've ever heard before."

"Hopefully we'll find them," Noah said. "I'd like to give you my contact information and get yours. I don't work specifically in trafficking, but I know the guys who do. I can get you in contact with them. The more information we have about who took them, where they were, what happened, the better able we'll be to stop them."

"Thank you." Dr. Terrell handed over a card, and Noah took a photo before shoving the card into his pocket.

"Miss Anderson," Dr. Terrell said. "If you need anything at all, I'm available."

"Thank you."

The doctor left, and Noah's phone rang. "I need to get this."

"Sure," Keeley said. "I should rest. I think they're letting me go in a bit."

Noah nodded as he swiped his finger over the screen and stepped out of the room. "Agent Grey."

"Noah, it's Cody. It looks like they've tracked down the owner of the house. They're going to make a move in about an hour. A surveillance team will be in the area in about five minutes. Hopefully, they'll be able to catch these guys before they can move."

"Thank God. I'm taking Keeley to my place when she is discharged. I'll be at the office as soon as I can."

"Take the day off, Long says so. Don't come in, I'm serious."

Noah resisted the groan he wanted to make. He didn't like skipping work, but Keeley would probably need him around. She had to be feeling off. His desire to work threatened to override his better instincts. Keeley would be upset. She had survived an ordeal. He would need to be with her, but he also wanted to hear everything they had on this case.

"I'll think about it."

"Good. And I'll keep you updated," Cody said.

"Sure. I'll text when we leave the hospital."

He went back into her room and found a nurse getting Keeley unhooked from the IV drip so she could leave.

"Hello," the nurse said when he walked in.

"That's Noah," Keeley flashed a smile that made his heart stop.

"Ah, the boyfriend. We're glad you're here. So Keeley will need to keep her bandages dry. She has a few wounds that will need to be looked at again. We're not going to make you drive all the way out here. You can go to your doctor in San Antonio. You're probably going to be sore. The doc said you don't have any broken ribs, but still, take it easy."

"I will," Keeley said.

"Good. Now then, just sign here and here, and I'll be back with a script for pain medicines and some antibiotics. We don't want that wound on your hand to get infected."

Noah moved closer to Keeley and put his hand on her arm. "Thank you."

The nurse gave a small smile and turned, leaving the room. Keeley looked uncomfortable.

Noah studied her for a moment before asking. "What's up?"

"Clothes. I don't really have any to wear."

"I have a change of clothes in my car. Let me go out and get them. I don't have any shoes, though."

The door opened, and Noah glanced over his shoulder. It was the nurse. "Shoes should be okay. We don't really want her wearing anything tight, so we have extra socks and these stylish boots that aren't comfortable and are impractical if you ask me, but they will work for getting you out to your car."

"So we have shoes covered. I'll grab a T-shirt and shorts out of my car. They may be a little big, but the shorts have a drawstring, and the T-shirt should at least be comfortable."

"Thank you, Noah." Keeley's gaze found his, and her smile lit up his soul. She really was different. He'd never felt these kinds of emotions she elicited. This woman changed everything for him.

He grabbed the clothes from his car and a sweatshirt in case she was cold. He'd received a text from Cody, telling him the surveillance team was in place. This was going to be a long night for the team, but if they found the asshole who was running the trafficking ring, it would be worth it.

The nurse drew the curtain around the bed, and Keeley changed into his T-shirt and shorts. When she stepped out from behind the curtain, wincing with each step, his heart shattered. He moved to her side.

"You should sit."

"I have to get used to it," she countered.

The door opened, and the nurse shot her a sharp look. "Sit down. No walking unless absolutely necessary. You'll be on your feet in no time, but they need to heal a little first."

"Okay, I get it." Keeley dropped to the chair and waited for the nurse to set up the wheelchair for her.

"Time to go," the nurse declared as she moved to help Keeley.

Noah made sure Keeley was stable as she stood and then slid into the wheelchair. It didn't take long, and they were in the car, ready to go. The drive home took less than an hour. Most of the traffic from the wreck had cleared though they still had one lane closed. He imagined it would take the rest of the night to clear out the few remaining cars.

Once at his place, he helped Keeley get settled after she used the restroom. She said she was fine sleeping in his shirt and honestly it looked so damn good on her he didn't want her to take it off.

They stretched out on his bed together. She seemed

nervous. Then he rolled to his side and placed his hand on her arm. She sighed.

"I like this." Keeley's whispered words worked through him, leaving him filled with desire.

"So do I. I like having you close."

"I think I'll be okay in a few days."

"You don't have to be. What happened was awful."

Keeley sighed and rolled to her side. "It was, but knowing you were out there looking for me, made it better."

"How did you know?"

Her fingers traced over his jawline. He moved in, kissing her lips before pulling back. He didn't want to go too deep and scare her away. The last thing he ever wanted was to make her leave.

"Because I trust you. I knew once you realized I was gone that you'd figure out a way to find me."

"It was terrifying thinking you were lost." He swallowed hard as emotions rose. "I know the stats. I'm thankful you're alive."

"Same here." Keeley yawned and closed her eyes.

He watched as she fell asleep. Having her beside him made everything better. Eventually, he wanted this to be permanent. He knew it was too early to hope they could move to this stage, but he wanted it to happen soon.

He woke before Keeley and left the room after brushing his teeth in the attached bathroom. While he poured coffee, he checked his texts. By the time the FBI arrived, the house Keeley had been kept in was empty. They found evidence of human trafficking, the buckets in the rooms that were used as toilets, the bloodstains, the smells, but no one was there. They were looking at more leads, praying the trail didn't grow cold.

He guessed the guy who had gotten away from the

wreck Keeley had been in had alerted the traffickers and they'd fled. It sucked that the other man hadn't been killed too. Normally he wouldn't wish death on anyone, but these were very bad people who were harming innocent men, women, and children.

Keeley woke a little after ten, and they headed out to grab breakfast since he didn't have much at home. They went by a bagel place with a drive-through and then dropped by her apartment for clothes and loose shoes.

She scheduled a doctor's appointment for the next day and took a nap while he caught up on work. Keeley planned on going into work the next morning. He wasn't too keen on her being away from him, but he needed to get back to work too.

Again, she spent the night, and he drove her to work the next day. When he showed up at the office, they were in full swing, searching for information on the human trafficking ring. He checked his emails and made sure there was nothing pressing he had to take care of before he jumped in tracking down leads on the traffickers.

Once again, they ruled out people and places but didn't actually find the human traffickers known as Amos and Mitchell. Frustration filled him.

At three he received a text from Keeley, saying she'd gone home to rest. Worry filled him when he called and didn't get an answer. He was about to race out the door when she called back.

"Keeley, where are you?" Panic filled his voice.

"I'm okay. I'm at home, and I'm going to rest for a while."

"Don't answer your door for anyone. I'm going to be here until about seven tonight."

"I'll be fine."

He groaned as he swiped his hand down his face. She would be okay. They didn't know where she lived, only where she worked. He hated this. They had to find the men responsible.

"I'll call before I come over."

"Thank you for everything," Keeley said.

"Hey, I care about you. I'll be there tonight, and we can stay at your place or go to mine."

Her laughter surprised him. He was about to say something when she spoke. "Your place is so much more comfortable than mine. I still have a small bed, and I don't think both of us will fit."

Heat shot from his heart to his cock. He blew out a breath, forcing himself to calm. "Sounds good. I'll call before I pick you up."

Her laughter went deeper and made his balls pull up. "I guess that means you want to sleep with me again?"

"Oh yes." He glanced up, seeing his boss approaching. "Sorry, gotta go."

"Okay, I'll talk to you later."

"Noah, we're researching a new lead," Long said. "Want to join us in the main conference room?"

"Yes, ma'am. I'll be right there."

"How is Keeley?" Long asked.

"She's doing okay. I think once these guys are caught, she'll be great."

"Good," Long said. "Now we just have to catch them."

Noah spent the rest of the afternoon and into the evening tracking leads that went nowhere. At six-fifty he left work and headed to Keeley's apartment. When he was about a block away, he called her. She hadn't answered by the time he pulled into the lot, and worry filled him. What if something had happened to her?

CHAPTER FIFTEEN

Keeley headed out to grab a burger. Walking was slow, but she didn't want to pay for another Uber ride. Her cash was being stretched thin. It sucked not being able to work when she needed the money so badly. She still had to finish filling out the forms for college. She prayed she received a scholarship because everything that had happened had changed her perspective on life and what she wanted from it.

The people she worked with were friendly, but her dream was to work at a museum or gallery. She loved the history of art and how those tiny little facts about an artist could change the way people viewed the piece and maybe even the world around them.

She'd finished half her burger at the restaurant and wrapped the rest up, deciding to eat it at home. Her appetite wasn't back yet, which the doctor said may happen. Spending a few days starving had changed how her body worked. The pain also cut her appetite.

The sun was still up, though it was sinking fast. Traffic had begun to taper from the after-work crowd. The area where she lived wasn't the best, but it wasn't terrible. She didn't want to freak out from walking a few blocks in the middle of the day.

A van drove past slowly, and she shivered. Unease filled her. It was evening, and the sun had almost gone down. The shadows were long and would allow someone to hide in their dark recesses. She pushed away the fear and continued on her way home. She was almost there when her phone started ringing. She moved the bag of food over to her other hand when the van she'd gotten the odd feeling about pulled up beside her and stopped.

Real fear took hold. The van door opened and she recognized one of the men. The urge to run hit hard. She dropped the bag of food and took off, hobbling away too slowly to really escape them.

Her building was up ahead, and she turned the corner, seeing Noah. She waved her hand and started screaming.

Noah was smiling at first, but his smile turned into a frown when he drew closer. Concern was evident on his face.

"What's wrong?" he asked.

She pointed behind her. "The guys. They were just there."

"The ones who had you?"

"Yes." The word came out as a sob. "They were in a black van."

"Shit." He walked past her and moved around the corner. Keeley followed.

"They're gone." Her voice shook as she spoke.

Noah pulled out his phone and dialed someone. "It's Agent Grey. A black van just tried to abduct Keeley." Noah turned to her. "No, she's safe." Noah nodded. "Yes, I think that's a great idea." Noah hung up and shoved his phone in his pocket before running his hands through his hair.

"What's a great idea?"

"They know where you live. We're close, but not close enough to finding them. Cody has a friend with a cabin outside of Houston. We're going to stay there for a while."

Panic filled her. "But my job."

"You'll be dead if you stay here."

She closed her eyes and held him close. Her sigh was heavy. "Okay, okay. I think you're right. I'll go with you. I just...I hate bailing on my job again."

"You didn't bail last time, and if you get abducted again, they won't have you around at all. You can't work if you're being trafficked to some asshole in Austin."

"True."

"Let's get some of your stuff and go. We need to swing by my place then we're going to take an FBI car and head out."

She was quiet as they went inside and packed a bag. She brought enough clothes for a week and a few things that would make her more comfortable. Being alone with Noah for a few days would be an interesting test of their relationship.

Once packed, she stepped into the den and met Noah's gaze. Trepidation filled her. "Are you really okay with this?"

"Yes. We need to keep you safe. I can do all my work where we'll be since most of it is on the phone talking to agencies. I'll set up meetings for next week and do computer work, so it won't be that big of a deal not being here." Her brows lifted as he spoke. "What's that look for?"

"I don't know what I'll do."

"Finish applying for school and get a start on reading for the first classes."

"That's smart." Keeley lifted up and kissed his cheek, which turned a cute shade of pink. "I think you liked that."

His lips curved up as he met her gaze. "I did. I'm going to enjoy spending time with you."

She grabbed her computer on the way out and gave one last look around her sad apartment. It wasn't much, but it had been home for a while. She pushed away thoughts of home and all the bad feelings that brought up and stepped outside with Noah, ready to move forward. Maybe home didn't have to be negative. With Noah she could reframe the word, making it theirs. She imagined with this man, home would mean warmth and happiness.

She thought of her parents, wondering for a moment if they had anything to do with this? No, her dad hadn't been into trafficking humans, only drugs. Plus, the guys who'd stored the drugs at Doc Julian's place had abducted her, not business partners of her dad.

That night they stayed at a hotel with two armed officers guarding their rooms. She couldn't wait to get to the location where they were going to be staying. Noah hadn't told her where they were headed because he didn't want her to have the weight of keeping quiet about where they were going.

The next morning they started their drive, heading out of town on I10. They were almost to Houston when Noah finally told her where they were traveling to.

"The cabin we're headed to is near Dayton Lakes. It's a small community, unknown to others because a friend of Agent Cody Whittaker owns it. It's the perfect location to hide. Plus they have great internet speed at the place. We'll have peaceful nights and days, and you can even sit outside and enjoy the sun. If we stayed here, I would fear you being outside at all."

"Why do you think they're after me?"

"No clue, it could have been the cop you saw them kill or the kids who were still in the house. Or it could be something else."

"Well, I'm glad I'm spending time with you."

He took her hand squeezing before letting go and grabbing the steering wheel. They stopped in Houston for lunch then by the grocery store once they were closer to their final destination.

The area was rural. It had been a long time since she'd been out of the city. The sky was clear, the air crisper. Once at the cabin, they unloaded then she laid down for a rest while Noah checked his email. That evening, Noah grilled steaks for them while she made rice and a salad. They ate on the back patio, sipping wine she'd insisted they pick up. The sun had gone down, and the silence had descended. There were bug and frog noises, but it was nothing like the sounds of the city, hundreds of thousands of people, airplanes, vehicles, and other sounds from living so close. This was peaceful.

Keeley set her wine glass on the table and stared up at the stars. "It's nice."

"It is, but I have to say just being with you is enough. If we were in San Antonio, or here, being with you is better than anything I've ever experienced."

She chuckled. "You're going to make me feel self-conscious. I'm not that good."

"But you are." He reached out and took her hand. "You're strong. You may not think you are, but you are. You've been through so much."

The fear and pain came back in a flash. This was part

of the post-traumatic stress the doctors had talked about. Noah stood and pulled her up too.

"I didn't mean to make you feel nervous or upset."

She shrugged. "It's okay."

"No, not really. I don't like you being upset." He wrapped both arms around her and began moving slowly like they were dancing. It was nice just being with him. They may not have forever, but they had right now.

Noah carried their glasses, and Keeley took the plates. Once inside, Noah took the dishes from her and placed them in the sink, rinsing them to get the food off. He turned to her, his expression serious.

"I want to kiss you."

She swallowed and nodded. "Sure."

His lips twitched up. "You sure? That's all?"

She shook her head. "No. I want to strip off your shirt and see how big and solid your muscles are. Then I want to take off your pants and explore your hard cock."

"Oh God, I wasn't expecting you to say that."

"Problem?" she asked.

"Hell no. I just wasn't expecting you to be ready."

"I want to kiss you everywhere. I want to suck you in and listen to you scream as you orgasm. I need your cock in me."

He pressed her up against the wall and stared into her eyes, looking like he was taking measure before he kissed her long and hard. Their lips mashed together, and though it was obvious he was trying to be gentle, his hands on her sides were painful, but she needed to feel him. She needed to feel him branding her with his love.

The kiss ended, and he stepped back. "I've been in these clothes all day. I want to shower first, then I want to take you in my arms and make love to you."

"Let's shower together."

She saw the shiver snake over his body.

"That's the best idea ever."

He led her upstairs to the loft and the shower. They hastily stripped, keeping their eyes on each other. Keeley smiled as Noah revealed himself. His muscles were beautiful, and the fuzz on his chest only made him look better. She moved in close and reached out, touching the line of hair that ran down the middle of his body.

His dick was hard, and she wanted to please him. Her gaze raked over his abs and then up to his chest and finally, his face. Heat filled her, and he pulled her close, his lips trapping her. The kiss was fiery and filled with passion.

Noah moved them to the bathroom and flipped on the water. They both stepped in and yelped at the cool water that soon turned hot. Then his hands were on her, smoothing soap over her shoulders and down to her breasts. His fingers ran over her nipples then back over them again. He met her gaze as he squeezed one nipple then the other.

"You're so sexy," he growled.

She leaned in, nuzzling his neck. "I think you're sexy." Her eyes went to his cock again. She needed to feel him.

He slid the soap lower and washed her belly, then his hands dipped even lower and ran over the top of her pubic bone. He groaned and leaned in, pulling her closer as soap slicked fingers slid between her folds, finding her bundle of nerves. He stroked over her clit, bringing her pleasure. She held on to him, her body vibrating with lust and passion as he took her higher.

"I'm going to make you come." The sexy growl from Noah pushed her over the edge. It had been so long since anyone had touched her. She came hard and fast, her body pulsing from his touch.

He held her with one arm while he washed his body, moving fast with the soap over his muscles. She stepped back, watching as he rinsed. She took the bar from the soap tray and washed under her arms and the rest of her body before running one soap covered hand over his length.

Noah jerked back, gasping as she stroked him. "Oh God, I'm going to blow if you keep touching me."

"Isn't that the goal?"

"No, I want to be inside you, buried deep, connected with you. I'll wear a condom, but soon I want to go without."

"I'm not on the pill."

"You're not?" He blinked at her, confusion evident on his face.

"It's not like I have sex that often and it messes with me. I haven't found anything that works. I mean, I can test some out, but when I was younger, it wasn't good for me."

"Okay, so we'll figure something out. But you're not a virgin, right?"

Embarrassment twisted through her. "Might as well be. It's been over a year."

"Oh."

She hesitated and leaned back a little. "You okay with that?"

"I am. I was just thinking of picking you up and taking you in here, but I think the bed might be better with some slow action first."

"I'm good with either. It's been so long. I just want to feel."

Noah leaned in, his lips were by her ear, his breath warming her. "I'll make sure you feel."

He shut off the water and handed her a towel before grabbing one for himself. The fear of rejection started to weave into her thoughts, and she held the towel so it covered her body.

"What are you doing?" Noah's intense gaze drilled into her.

"I just...It's weird being naked in front of you."

"Weird how?"

"I don't want to disappoint you."

Noah pulled her to him, his arms wrapping around her, protecting her. "Oh baby, you won't disappoint me."

"But what if—"

His lips were on hers, his tongue invading. He walked them into the bedroom then they were both on the bed, he stretched out beside her, the towel forgotten somewhere on the way.

His fingers splayed out over her belly, his warmth filling her belly. The kiss ended, and he went up on one elbow and stared down at her like he was drinking her in.

"You are perfect for me. I don't want you to ever doubt that."

She was about to answer when he lowered his head and sucked her nipple into his mouth. She arched up, needing more than just his mouth on her breast. He didn't disappoint. His fingers roamed over her body, touching, squeezing, fanning flames that heated her.

When Noah kissed a path down her torso to her core, she came unglued. His tongue licked over her clit, and then he sucked it in. Her fingers buried in his hair and she held him there as he took her back to bliss.

His hand was at her opening, and he slid in two fingers. The invasion felt good. He didn't bang away at her like some idiot with a jackhammer. Instead, he moved slowly, loving her, making everything feel so damn perfect.

The good feelings spread. Keeley arched off the bed

again, coming around his fingers. He didn't move as she rode out her orgasm, giving her time to recover. Then he was on her, his lips tasted like her, and she moaned as he slid his tongue in, fucking her mouth.

The kiss ended, and she thought Noah was leaving her when he rolled away, but he grabbed the condom off the table by the bed and opened the package. She noticed his hands were shaking.

He met her gaze and shot her a wicket hot smile. "I can't wait to sink into you."

"Noah," was all she could manage.

He moved fast and was between her legs, pulling them up to wrap around his waist. As he positioned himself, he held her gaze. It felt as if their souls touched as he slid in, filling her up.

His fingers had felt good, but his cock was huge, and she gulped in a breath as she fought to keep from spiraling out of control.

His body brushed against hers, and the base of his cock grazed against her clit. She cried out, and lifted, trying like crazy to get even closer to him. She wanted every inch of him touching her.

Noah pulled out slowly then slid back in an unhurried pace, driving her wild. Again, the base of his cock grazed her sensitive clit, making her see sparks.

By the wicked grin on his face, he knew what he was doing. Noah kept up the torturous measured pace, leaving her so close to orgasm she would do anything to come again.

He lowered so his lips were close to her ear as he whispered. "Want to come?"

"God, yes. Please." She wasn't above begging.

"Flip over."

"What?" Confusion filled her.

"Trust me."

He pulled out, and she flipped over. She was about to spread her legs when he straddled her and lifted her hips a little. Then he moved off her and grabbed a pillow.

"Put the pillow under you to lift your hips."

"Okay."

She did as he asked, and then he was straddling her again. The urge to spread her legs hit, but he had her trapped. Then his cock was sliding against her legs, and she felt him at her vagina. He pushed in, filling her. The friction was higher. She pushed her hips up and back. He caressed her bottom, sending warmth through her.

The movement, the shock, his cock sliding in all came together in a conflagration of lust. He was so big and she felt every inch of him this way. She gasped for breath and pushed back. His hand came around and stroked her clit. It was all she needed. Keeley came harder than ever before. She gasped for breath as her body gripped down on Noah's cock. She wanted the condom gone, his seed spilling into her. The desire to be everything to him, to be his one and only took over her mind, erasing any rational thoughts.

Noah's chest was plastered against her back, his breath harsh as he bucked above her. She was still pulsing around him when he sat up and pulled out before flopping down next to her.

She turned so she could stare at him. This man had totally and completely changed everything. His fingers trailed over her cheek and chin before running gently over her back.

"Did I hurt you?"

She shook her head. "No. I'm still sore, but hurting, no. That was amazing."

His lips crooked up in a smile. "It felt good."

"Holy hell, you made me come three or four times tonight."

"I want you to feel good."

Laughter escaped her lips. "Oh, I feel good. That's for sure."

He kissed her before sitting up. She watched him remove the condom and head to the bathroom. Then he was back, pulling her into his arms. He kissed her lips and her cheeks before he kissed her forehead and sighed.

"I hate the reason why where here, but I like being here with you."

She nodded. "It's nice spending time in your arms. I like this."

"So, about school?"

She groaned. "I still don't have the money and won't."

"What if you did? I mean, what if you did get a scholarship and a few grants and maybe a loan."

"I still have to pay for rent and food, and everything else. Living is expensive."

Noah stiffened. "I know it's crazy, and I'm crazy for suggesting it, but what if you moved in with me?"

Her throat went dry. They lay there for a full minute, maybe more. Everyone she knew would tell her not to say yes. She knew better, but what if he had a point.

"It would be hard," she finally said.

"I know." He sat up and flipped on the bedside lamp. His expression was serious as he focused on her. "I have a two-bedroom apartment. If you wanted to move in as a roommate first while we date. We could have rules."

"We just fucked like porn stars. Do you think we'd follow those rules?"

"Yes."

She threw back her head, laughing at the thought of

them keeping their hands off each other. When she met his gaze again, he didn't seem insulted or angry. Instead, he was smiling.

"The sex was freaking hot, that would be hard to stop doing, but I think we could come up with some solution."

She narrowed her eyes and hit him with a pointed stare. "A solution that includes sex, right?"

He laid down and pulled her close. "Yes, a solution that includes sex."

Being with Noah was different. He treated her differently than boyfriends in her past had treated her. He wasn't rude or dismissive. He seemed like he really wanted this to work between them. And he was still here, in bed with her after they'd had awesome sex, holding her close while cuddling.

She wanted to live with him, but the fear of him getting tired of her held her back from agreeing to the plan. She liked the idea, but she'd learned from her family that having good intentions didn't mean the person backing up that idea was actually into following through with the plan.

Moving in with Noah might work, but it also might be the worst idea ever.

CHAPTER SIXTEEN

Noah woke hard and wanting. Keeley was already out of bed. He was surprised he hadn't heard her get up. After a quick shower, and scrub with his toothbrush, he headed into the kitchen where she had two eggs hot out of the pan for him along with coffee, fresh fruit, and bacon.

"Wow, this looks great."

"Good. I've been up for a while, so I already ate."

"Couldn't sleep?" he asked as he settled at the table.

"It's too quiet."

Her laughter filtered over him, leaving him thinking he really had scored big when he'd met her.

"I need to work today. What are your plans?"

"I have my computer now. I'm going to finish filling out the applications for scholarships and call them to check on the progress of my application. I want to make sure I get into the next semester, even if it is just for a few classes."

"Good. I'll make us lunch when we break."

She moved behind him and held onto his shoulders. Her hands felt good on him. "There's no need. I'll probably be bored by then anyway. I need to find some art history stuff and catch up on what I've missed in the last few years."

"I'll help you make lunch. I don't want food preparation to only fall on you."

Keeley stepped around to one of the empty chairs, a white coffee cup in her hand as her lips twisted, making her look even more adorable than he thought she was. Of course, he didn't tell her that she was adorable because he didn't want her thinking he was patronizing her.

"You're being nice."

He shrugged. "This is how I am."

"So after a few months of dating, you're not going to go all caveman on me and expect me to fix all your meals?"

He sighed and took a sip of coffee. "I've run into this before."

Keeley lifted her eyebrows. "Really?"

"Yes. I've dated, and I once lived with a woman in Virginia. It didn't work out."

"I'm sorry."

He blinked at Keeley. "You really mean that, don't you?"

"What, that I'm sad you had to go through having a relationship that broke up? Of course, I'm not happy you went through that. It had to have been painful."

"You really are a good person," Noah said.

"So are you." Keeley rested her chin on her hands. "So about the meal thing, what were you saying?"

"She didn't get that I really didn't want a slave. I want a partner. That means we both take a share of the work. If I'm home, I can start laundry. With work, I may be gone. I can't help that. Just like if you have a late class, I'm certainly not waiting to have dinner just because you're busy. I've known some men who demanded their wife be home at six each evening to fix him a meal. I've always thought that was rather asinine. You could have something going on, and why couldn't he cook for her. Lazy is lazy, whether it's man or woman. You share in the tasks, that's what makes a relationship. If one person is the ruler, it doesn't work. People may think it does, but it doesn't. There's always someone manipulating the situation if they don't feel they have an equal say."

Keeley laughed, and for a second, he thought she was laughing at him. Then she dried her eyes and met his stare.

"Sorry, but you nailed it. My mom used to manipulate my dad so much. It took me years to see it. If you'd met them back then, you would have probably seen it first off. They were terrible together. Of course, they broke the law and embezzled money and cheated people and did all sorts of other illegal things, so why shouldn't they manipulate each other." She wiped her eyes again, still laughing. "I don't mean to laugh, but if I take what my parents did too seriously, I'll cry. But being with you, I now have hope."

He swallowed his forkful of eggs and picked up another bite. "What kind of hope?"

"That I can get my degree. It might take longer, but if I don't do this now, I'll be thirty and regretting my decision to not get this done. I don't want to find myself in my fifties, miserable because I didn't do this. Maybe I'll hate working in a museum or gallery, but I think I'll love it."

He reached out and took her hand. "Did you know they have a group of FBI agents who deal with art crime? Then there's teaching, and working for companies, doing design, I bet there's a lot of different jobs you could get with a master's in art history. But first, you have to get it."

"Art history and working for the FBI, that's a stretch."

"No, not really. I mean if you also did some criminal

justice classes and then art history, you'd be perfect for the job. Not that you want to take a job like that, but there are so many things that will open up to you if you go ahead and get the degree. And you may find that working in a museum is exactly what you want to do."

He dropped her hand and took another bite of eggs as she sipped her coffee. He could tell he'd given her a lot to think about.

"Okay, I'll give you that. You're right. I need to get a degree. I wish I could work in a museum without my masters, but they need to make sure you really know your stuff. I love art history anyway, so it really won't be a chore to study it."

"Who is your favorite artist?"

Keeley sat back and shrugged. "That's hard. You have to look past the beauty of the paintings to the depths of pain in their lives. The traditional Michael Angelo and da Vinci, along with Picasso, van Gogh, and Rembrandt, those are easy. I love Georges Seurat's work, but also Georgia O'Ke-effe. There's something that calls to me in their work. The key is not to get distracted by the giants of art, but to look beyond and find those who were great, but highly underrated."

"I've heard of O'Keeffe."

"I'm sure you have. She's an American."

"So what do you think of the modern trend to do shock art?"

Keeley shrugged and grabbed her coffee mug as she hopped up. "Sometimes, I find it hard to take them seriously."

"What do you mean?"

He'd finished his eggs and bacon, and Keeley grabbed

his plate and took it over to the sink where she washed it off.

"I get that artists want to be unique, but they are losing their uniqueness by trying to out-unique the last person."

"Like a single chair in the middle of the room?"

"Yes. Exactly. There has to be more than just placing a chair in an awkward position. What did they do to create? I mean if the person actually built the chair, sanded the wood, made the cushions, painted the wood, okay, that's great, but just placing a chair from Ikea in a room shouldn't qualify as art."

"You're very passionate about art. I'd love to go to New York or DC with you and look through a museum."

She laughed again, the sound refreshing. "I'd be annoying. I know too much to just walk through. It would be an educational experience, not necessarily an enjoyable experience."

"I think it would be enjoyable."

"We should start small, maybe the art museum in Houston first. That way, you could see just how annoying I am."

"I think you're adorable."

Keeley lifted her eyebrows. "Adorable?"

"Yeah, you're cute. I think you're very cute and I like you."

"I like you too."

"Good, so you'll move in?"

"Wow, you jumped into that very quickly."

He stood and pulled her into his arms. "I think we'll be good together. Yes, I'm impatient. Nearly losing you was too much. I can't stand the idea of you getting away because I didn't let you know how I felt about you."

"How do you feel?"

"Like if I don't have you in my arms, I'll fall on my face."

She cupped his cheeks and stared into his eyes. Could she trust him? Heck, could she trust herself? "I don't want to lose myself in any relationship."

He nodded. "I get that. I don't want you to let go of who you are. I like the you I've found, the person who makes me laugh and makes me think. I like who I am when I'm with you."

His phone rang, killing the mood instantly. He took a step back and grabbed his phone from his pocket, looking at the display.

"Work."

Keeley nodded as he left the room and headed into the study where he'd planned on working. The large desk was a little outdated, and the room was a bit musty, but a good cleaning would change that.

"Agent Noah Grey here."

"Noah, it's Cody. We're closing in on another location in a few hours. You may be able to come back this evening."

"That's great." His heart sank. He didn't want to go back to San Antonio, where they would have to face reality. He liked being here where he could pretend Keeley wanted to live with him. It was too soon to have her move in, and he knew it, but that didn't stop him from wanting her with him all the time.

"I'll send you the information once we take the guy down. This time, I think we have them."

"That's great. Thank you for calling. I hope this is it."

He hung up and dropped to the chair. Would it really be this easy? They could go back, and then what would happen? He and Keeley had had amazing sex, and he wanted her in his apartment, but he could see her saying no because she didn't want to intrude.

Of course, if they found the guy, then hopefully they would find the kids suffering at his hands. Those poor people. How many women and children had this asshole pushed into slavery. That's what human trafficking was. It wasn't just transporting someone; it was slavery plain and simple. Children were forced into sex slavery or working for companies, making little to no money.

He stood up and headed back into the den. Keeley had her computer out at the table. He moved behind her and put his hands on her shoulders.

She glanced up, worry wrinkling her brows. "Everything okay?"

"It will be. It was Cody saying they were going to raid another location. We might be able to return home tonight."

"Oh."

He chuckled. "Yeah, I don't want to leave either."

She stood and wrapped her arms around his waist. "I like spending time with you. I think we could come up with a solution when we head home. My lease is up in two months, so I was probably going to move anyway. I don't know where, but I'd need somewhere to live."

His breath caught as excitement filled him. "Seriously, move in with me."

She hesitated which made him hold his breath. "How far do you live from the dentist's office?"

Excitement filled him. She was thinking about it. "Not far."

"My car was totaled, but it's not enough money from the insurance to buy a new car. I don't know what I'm going to do."

"First off, finish working on your application to school.

We'll figure it all out. Something good will come up, I know it."

She nodded and glanced to her computer, then back to him. "Okay, I'll get my application in and start looking at what is required in the firsts classes I need to take, and you go work. We'll meet back up at lunch."

"Sounds good to me."

Noah leaned in and brushed his lips over hers. She tasted like morning and hope. Soon, they would really be living together instead of just hanging out together at some cabin. He couldn't wait until she was his and their life together had really begun.

CHAPTER SEVENTEEN

THE RAID HADN'T PANNED OUT. NOTHING IN SAN Antonio seemed to be accomplishing anything that would end the nightmare of having to hide from the gang who wanted to sell her. She'd filled out applications, scholarship forms, submitted paperwork, did the forms for grants, took care of everything she needed to do, and figured out what classes she needed to take. Everything from Columbia would transfer.

She would have to take art and architecture of Europe and the New World, but then she'd be able to move into more specific upper-level classes. The program excited her. She figured she could take two classes a semester to start with unless she got a full scholarship, then she could go to school full time.

By the third afternoon, she was bored and ready to do something other than sitting around the cabin. Not too far into town, if you could call the place with one stop sign and a gas station, a town, there was a store. She needed to do something other than sit around. Her feet had healed fast.

She wouldn't be running around barefoot outside, but she could walk in shoes no problem.

She moved to the door and heard Noah on the phone. Instead of bugging him, she left the house and started the trek to the store. She wasn't moving fast, which was fine by her because it gave her time to look at the trees and study the sky.

Once in town, she bought a soda and an ice cream. She thought about picking up a magazine, but they were expensive. Before turning back to the cabin, she walked around the four blocks that made up the town. There wasn't anything to the place. It was small with few houses, and it was a wonder the gas station and store stayed in business. She guessed it was the lake traffic that kept the place running.

About a half-mile from the cabin, she saw Noah race out of the house to his car. She waved, not at all thinking anything of him running out to the car. He paused and then ran toward her. Anger masked his features.

"What the heck are you doing?"

She stopped, unsure how to answer his question. Why was he so angry?

"Why are you out here?" he demanded.

"I-I just walked into town." She narrowed her gaze, trying to figure out what was wrong with him.

"Hell." He grabbed her arm and dragged her toward the house.

She wrenched away from him. "Hey, that hurts. What is wrong with you?"

"With me? With me? You left the house. You can't leave."

Anger filled her up. "I didn't realize I was a prisoner."

Noah threw his hands up in the air and growled. "You aren't a prisoner. My God, you have someone who wants to take you away and make you a sex slave. You can't walk around like this."

She opened her arms and turned around slowly. "We're in the middle of freaking nowhere. No one is out here."

"Damn." Noah pulled her into a hug. She noticed he was shaking, and she leaned back, staring into his eyes.

"I'm okay."

"God, you scared the shit out of me. I think I might have crapped my pants."

She studied him, noticing the sweat on his brows and the pinched skin around his mouth. "I'm sorry. I wasn't thinking. We're here, and nothing else is happening."

He pulled her into a hug. "I was so scared." His voice cracked. She didn't dare pull back and look to see if he was crying. She hadn't thought about the danger of walking to the store or walking around the town. Then it hit, she'd grown complacent. She hadn't even thought about the guys trying to get her.

Noah loosened his hold on her and she glanced up at him, her lips trembling with emotions.

"I felt so safe here with you. I'm sorry."

He blew out a breath and shook his head. "I overreacted. I was just so worried. I can't lose you. I don't think you understand how I feel about you."

She cupped his cheek. "I won't go out alone again."

"Good. I don't want to have to lock you up."

She lifted her eyebrows and looked doubtfully at him. "You wouldn't."

He slung one arm around her shoulder and led her back to the cabin. "Don't tempt me. I just want to keep you safe."

She snorted and placed her hand on his chest. "Do you really think there's anything that can keep me safe?"

"Yes, me."

Her gaze met his. A smile stretched her lips wide. "You're very confident."

"I am. And that's what makes me good. I know I can take a guy down with a gun. I've trained for years to protect people like you. I said I would keep you safe, and I will."

They stopped outside the house. She lifted her hands so she had hold of his face. "I'm sorry. I didn't think going into this little town would make any difference. If we go home, I don't want to be locked up. I'll want to go to work and school."

He blew out a breath. "If we catch these guys, you'll be able to."

"Even if we don't catch them, I can't be a prisoner."

He nodded, but she wasn't sure he understood she would never be the type of person to sit back and let other people take care of her. She'd done that before with her parents, and it hadn't worked out so well.

"Just promise me you'll tell me where you're going." His voice was low, sexy, and drew her to him. "I can't keep you safe if I don't know."

Her breath hitched as emotions filled her up. "You can't keep me safe if you do know. No one is safe."

He shot her a look like she was crazy. "You do know I'm FBI. Anyone comes at you, and I'm around then you can bet I'm taking them down."

"But what if—"

"No, please don't what if me. I know life can be difficult and things happen, I just need to know you're safe, even if it is a false illusion, just something to keep me from going crazy."

She put her hand on his chest and moved a step closer. "I promise. I didn't mean to scare you. Now then, let's go back inside and keep the neighbors from talking."

He waggled his eyebrows. "At least there aren't many neighbors around here."

Keeley looked around. "Nope, there aren't. It's weird."

"What?"

"I've lived in the city for most of my life, in the burbs mostly, but now I'm inside the city, and there is always noise. This is different."

Noah glanced around. "It is. It's peaceful."

A small shiver snaked down her spine. "And a little odd. I walked around the town—"

"Don't remind me."

"Nothing happened, just chalk it up as my one screw up, okay."

Noah stopped walking. "You didn't screw up, I did."

She shook her head. "No, I was the one who left."

"But you are in my charge right now. I'm responsible for your protection. If something happened to you, I would be held responsible."

"Wait, what?" She caught his gaze. "That's not right."

He shrugged. "Right or wrong, I'm the one who is here, and if something happens, I'll have to explain what happened and how."

"I don't like that."

"Would you rather be stuck in a house with someone else?"

Her lips thinned and she moved to him then wrapped her arms around his waist. "Oh no, I only want to be stuck in a house with you."

He lifted his eyebrows. "Have you been bored?"

She rolled her eyes and took off toward the house. "So freaking bored."

"We should have sex again."

She spun and walked backward to the door. "First one naked gets top."

His lips spread into the sexy smile she loved. "You'd best start getting undressed if you want the top."

She tugged open the door and slipped in, tossing her shirt and her bra on the floor as she reached for her pants, shoving them and her underwear low in one quick move.

"Tada! Totally naked," Keeley said as she watched Noah tug at the button of his shirt. He'd had a video call today, so he had to wear a tie and he wasn't stripping fast. She laughed as she moved up the stairs to the bed, thinking about how she wanted him.

About thirty seconds later, he came racing up the stairs, his cock hard. She lifted her brows and pointed to the bed.

"What are you planning?" Noah asked.

"Sucking you and then riding you."

Noah's cheeks were pink, and he looked ready for sex. His cock was hard, his face flushed. His eyes were dark with lust, and his cheeks were pink.

She grabbed a condom before she moved to the bed. Being with Noah was fun. She liked how he treated her and how he acted. It would be easy to live with him.

"You okay with me riding you?"

"Oh yeah. I want to watch you on me."

She moaned and moved fast, wrapping her lips around his cock. He cried out and arched up. She didn't let up until he started begging. Then she covered him with a condom and moved into position, guiding him into her pussy as she lowered.

His eyes were bright, and his expression intense. His lips curled up in a feral grin. He looked dangerous, but she knew he was the same sweet man who had rescued her. Noah was the right man for her, she had little doubt about that. If only they'd known each other for longer, then the question about moving in with him wouldn't be an issue because she'd be at his doorstep, ready to declare herself a member of his household.

He grabbed her hips and lifted her before pushing her down while his hips rose. His movements drove them faster, making her heat more. She was about to come. Her rhythm was floundering as he pushed her to a brutal pace.

She cried out and came just before he shot his cum into the condom. After she finished, she dropped low, resting her head on his shoulder.

He brushed the hair away from her face, delivering sweet little kisses. His dick shrunk and she knew she had to move so the condom wouldn't fall off, but it felt so good to lay with him. After another moment, she rolled to the side, wishing they could stay connected. He stood, the muscles of his legs highlighted in the sun streaming in as he walked away. This man was perfect for her.

She laid in bed, staring at the ceiling as thoughts of the last week hit her. How had she gone from working as a dental assistant to living in a cabin, hiding from someone who wanted to sell her as a sex slave? Heck, how had she gone from the woman at Columbia to a dental assistant? But if she hadn't moved back home, would she have ever met Noah. Were they fated to be together or had she met him by accident?

He stepped into the room from the bathroom, his sexy smile making her heart trip. She was glad she knew this man. She wouldn't have wanted life to be any other way.

Noah was hers, and she was his, they just had to get to that point in their relationship where declaring her love wouldn't be so awkward. She prayed they found the jerk who had held her then sold her, because living with that threat over her head was exhausting.

CHAPTER EIGHTEEN

THE CALL CAME IN AT THREE THE NEXT MORNING. Noah wasn't going to answer his phone, but he figured it was important for someone from work to be ringing him in the middle of the night.

"Agent Noah Grey," he said as he sat up, wiping his face while he tried to figure out where he was.

"We got him."

Noah stumbled from bed and headed downstairs to the kitchen. "Him? You mean the guy who was trafficking people?"

"Yes, one of them. We got the one who went by Mitchell."

"What about the other one?" Noah asked.

"He wasn't there, but we did get this one. We think you two can come back now."

"Okay, after we get some more sleep."

"Sure. And call before you leave. We want to really make sure it's safe here."

He moaned something and hung up before stumbling back upstairs to bed. He stretched out with Keeley, falling to sleep quickly. He didn't wake until almost eight. Noah couldn't believe he'd slept so late, but he'd left his phone downstairs when Cody had called and he'd missed his alarm. He was lucky he'd woken on his own since he had a phone call scheduled for eight-thirty that he couldn't miss.

"Hey, sleepyhead," Keeley said as he came downstairs.

"Good morning, sexy." He kissed her before moving to the coffeepot, where he poured up a cup. The first sip was heaven.

Yesterday he'd been hard on Keeley, but she'd scared the crap out of him. He'd never lost anyone he was in charge of protecting. Even the lowlife scum bag killers who turned state's evidence, he'd protected without once slipping up. With Keeley, she was his kryptonite. He knew better than to blindly accept she would stay in the house, he should have told her there were rules, but he'd wanted her to like him. Being a dick who laid down the law wasn't how he wanted her to see him.

Keeley moved close and lifted up on her toes, kissing his chin. "What are you thinking about?"

"Cody called last night."

"Is that why your phone was down here?"

He nodded. "They have Mitchell in custody."

"What about Amos?"

He shook his head and took a sip of coffee. "They think it's safe to come back to the city. I don't. I don't like this. I don't like how Amos is still out there. We aren't sure it was Mitchell who tried to grab you in that van."

"At some point, I have to start living my life again. It's doubtful they'll come for me."

He set his mug on the counter and crossed his arms over his chest. "You're staying at my place, right?"

"Will I be allowed to go to the store?"

He sighed and rubbed his hand over the scratchy stubble on his jaw. "I know I can't keep you prisoner, but there are rules you'll have to follow to stay safe. I don't want to be a dick, but there are just certain things you'll have to do."

"Like?"

"We need to understand exactly what this group was doing. How deep does their organization go? Are they a network or different cells? Did these two guys run everything? Once we understand, we'll have a better idea of the risks. Then we can figure out how much freedom you can enjoy while still being safe."

"I'm not rich. I can't hire a personal bodyguard, and I have to work."

"I know." He grabbed his mug and drank more. "I also know your life is in danger. I don't like the two options that are floating around for us. You don't have the luxury of disappearing, and you shouldn't have to. You should be able to live your life and not worry about some a-hole trying to take you to be his sex slave. I'm sorry any of this happened."

Keeley cupped his cheek. "It's not your fault."

"No, but it is my fault for not laying out more rules for you to follow here. I know we're in the middle of nowhere, and it seems like we're safe. But these people are evil. You can't trust them to play fair at all. There is nothing fair about them."

The snort from Keeley was filled with frustration. "Okay, so I don't know how to handle that."

"Which is why there are rules. I know it sucks, but one of them will be not leaving the apartment without someone going with you. I'll drive you to work and pick you up."

Her brows wrinkled. "That's hardly fair to you."

"It's hardly fair to you to have to live with rules." He kissed the top of her head before taking another sip of coffee. "It's only for a short time. We just need more information."

Keeley nodded before stepping over to the stovetop. She flipped on a burner and grabbed the eggs from the refrigerator.

"Do you really think they'll keep coming back for me?"

"I don't know. Maybe." He pulled out his phone and looked at it, opening his email to see if anything more had come in. Of course, everyone who had worked on the operation last night would be in bed. He'd had it easy. The next all-nighter, he should expect to be in on. "I don't have any information, but they're all probably still asleep. They were up late."

She cracked two eggs and glanced over her shoulder. "Do you want two or three?"

"Two is fine. I have a call I have to be on in just a bit. Then I'll make a decision about what to do."

"Hey."

He looked up, searching her face for any anger, or mistrust. He'd screwed up, and now she knew he'd messed up with her.

"Thank you for all you're doing."

Guilt filled him. "I should be doing more."

She shook her head before turning back to the pan to flip the eggs. "You seem disappointed. But Noah, you're doing more than most."

He rolled his eyes. "You left the house, and I didn't even know. I should have—"

"Stop. Will you. I know now. I should have thought about it, but I felt safe. You make me feel safe. Thank you."

His heart squeezed as guilt filled him. If he only made Keeley feel safe and she wasn't safe, then he would have failed. Keeley plated the eggs and handed it to him. Her smile warmed him, but the cold, clawing feeling of failure was in the background, taunting him. He had to do better, or he might just lose her forever.

CHAPTER NINETEEN

KEELEY DIDN'T LIKE THE GUILT SHE SAW IN NOAH'S eyes. He shouldn't feel bad about her mistakes. She'd screwed up going to town when she knew someone was after her. She should have stayed at the cabin and waited for him to be finished with his call.

The door to the office where Noah had been working opened, and he stepped out. "I talked to my boss, and they believe it's safe for you to come back. I still think you should live at my place."

She chuckled. "Is that your way of getting me to move in?"

"Maybe." He tilted his head and looked at her through his long eyelashes. The man was freaking sexy. She liked how he teased her and the way his smile made her heart beat faster.

"So if I do move in with you, we really have to keep the channels of communication open."

"I agree. And I don't want you to feel pressured to sleep with me."

She closed the distance between them and put her

hand on his chest. "I have no intention of sleeping anywhere else."

His lips spread into a sexy smile. "I'm so lucky to have found you."

"I think I'm the lucky one here. I mean really, if I hadn't known you, I still would have been abducted, but I wouldn't have been saved. No one would have come looking for me. I would still be held captive."

"You would have gotten away like you did. You are the one who rescued yourself."

She shook her head. "I don't know if I would have wanted to break free. You kept me going."

"Well, you keep me going," Noah said. "You make life worthwhile."

His words made her feel warm inside. Could she really be the type of person who made a difference in his life? Was he only saying that to make her feel better, or was it real?

His eyes narrowed and he frowned. "Don't doubt me."

Her brows pinched together. "You could tell I had doubts?"

"Yes, for some reason I can read what you're thinking. I mean, not always, but I can see that you don't believe what I said. You've made me better, I can't explain it, but I feel things more now."

She brushed her lips over his. "We have a lot going on between us. I want it to last."

"Me too." He wrapped his arms around her before pressing his lips to hers. She opened for him. He tugged off her shirt and pulled down her pants before backing her up against the wall.

His hands fumbled at the front of his pants, and then he

grabbed her leg under her knee and held it up as he slid into her.

"Condom," she gasped.

"Shit. I'm sorry. Give me a second."

She followed him into the bedroom and bend over the bed, exposing herself to him. His hands landed possessively on her hips. He didn't hesitate and slid in, pulling her butt back while he pushed forward.

Keeley gasped. She tried to breathe, but Noah shoved in again. He set a demanding pace that had her off balance. Her orgasm built as he pounded into her. The pleasure she achieved from him being rough was off the charts.

Then he pulled her up. His hands on her breasts, holding her in a mostly standing position as he thrust into her. The raw power coming from him was a potent aphrodisiac. She cried out as her orgasm hit. Then he clutched her close, his chest plastered against her back as he rocked into her and came.

One hand trailed down her body to her clit. His fingers worked magic, bringing her closer to another orgasm. When she was about to come, he pulled out, turned her around then pushed her to the bed. He was on her. His lips on her clit, sucking her in. She screamed as she came, the intensity too much to hold in.

When he sat up and looked down at her, lust coated his features. She reached for him, and he dropped to the mattress with her. This was heaven. She could get lost spending days in bed with him.

She ran her thumb over his lips. "That was freaking amazing."

"I thought so too." He kissed her cheek. "It wasn't too rough, was it?"

"Heck no. That was just right." A shiver worked through her, and he sighed.

"So you're going to sleep in my bed, right?"

A dark chuckle worked its way up and out. "Oh baby, I won't be sleeping anywhere else."

"Good, because I like this." His phone buzzed, and he groaned.

"You didn't even take off your pants, did you?" Keeley said.

His cheeks grew dark. "No." He read the text then turned to her. "I have this fantasy."

She lifted her brows and leaned back, staring at him. "What's it about?"

He swallowed hard. "The woman is wearing high heels and nothing else. I'm fully dressed in a suit and..."

"And you screw the woman without getting undressed?"

He nodded then glanced away. When he met Keeley's gaze again, he looked shy, like he wanted to ask her to fulfill his deepest fantasy but didn't know how.

She sat up, then looked back at him. "We'll see what we can do about that later. Maybe we can come up with some plan to play out your fantasies if you're willing to play out mine." She stood and moved toward the bathroom but was surprised to feel Noah's hand on her back. His eyes were wide when she turned to face him.

"Tell me about your fantasies."

She opened her mouth, but his phone rang. He groaned and reached down, buttoning and zipping his pants before he answered.

"Agent Noah Grey here."

She walked into the bathroom and shut the door. She needed to shower then she would help him pack up everything. They would be heading out soon. This little break from reality had been nice, but she had to go back to the real world. She prayed they could make it after they left, but her life wasn't easy or straightforward. It was nice to dream of college and living with Noah, but when the reality of life hit, she wasn't sure either dream would come true.

CHAPTER TWENTY

AFTER CLEANING THE CABIN AND TAKING THE TRASH to the municipal dump, they drove to San Antonio that afternoon. It was odd knowing she wasn't going to go back to her apartment. She didn't want to be a bother, but it seemed like Noah really wanted her around.

That night, they made love in his bed. It was soft and gentle, not like earlier. She liked both types of lovemaking, but she was interested in the fantasies Noah wanted to experience.

She was back at work the next day, which was odd. There were questions, but she kept the answers basic. Nothing was said in front of the patients.

At lunch, she checked her phone and saw she had a call from a number she didn't know. She sent a text to Noah, asking if he knew who it could be. He replied in minutes, stating it was someone from the university.

She dialed the number which was picked up on the second ring. "Hello, there was a message to call you on my phone. I'm Keeley Anderson."

"Yes, Miss Anderson. I'm so happy to hear back from

you. I'm Professor Dunwitty's assistant, Lila. We read over your essay, and we'd like for you to come in on Friday afternoon. This is about the full scholarship for art history majors who are coming back to school. We have hour-long appointments beginning at two until six. That last one is late, but Dunwitty knows people work."

"I get off on Friday at four forty-five or five. So I could be there at six."

"Good. I've marked you down for six."

"Do I need to bring anything?"

"Just any files you have from your previous course work. We're doing the evaluations for scholarships. Honestly, we both like you. There are three people on the committee evaluating the applicants."

"So there are four other applicants for the scholarship I'm applying for?"

"Oh no, there were eighty. We had phone interviews with twenty of the applicants. Dunwitty liked the conversation he had with you and used that for your interview. We looked at the courses you took at Columbia and your scores. We felt you exemplified what a true student of the arts is. There is one other person who is coming in for the interview. The other slots are for different scholarships."

"Oh." Her heart thundered as she imagined what her life would be like getting this scholarship. She'd looked into what the scholarship included and had been a little freaked out. It was too good to be true and she was sure she wouldn't get it. All of her course work, her books, her supplies, her food on campus, all if it would be covered and she would be given an eight hundred dollar a month stipend. If she lived with Noah, she may not actually have to work.

"I have you down, and I look forward to meeting you."

"Thank you. I can't wait until Friday."

She hung up and turned to find the dentist and the rest of the office staring at her. She put away her phone and cleared her throat.

"So that was the University of Texas San Antonio's art department. They are interviewing me for a full scholarship on Friday evening at six."

Doc Julian stepped forward, his eyebrows raised. "Like you'd get a full scholarship to go to school?"

She nodded, unable to keep the excitement inside. "I don't have it yet, but it's close. I met the Professor a few weeks ago, and I applied. I'm in the final running."

"Do you need to take time off?" Doc asked.

"No, the interview is at six."

"I'll drive you over," Sharron said. "I need to go out there and look at the campus. Daniel, my oldest, is seventeen. I think it would be good if he went there."

"Are you sure?" Keeley asked Sharron.

"Yes, I'm positive. I'm happy for you."

She felt like she'd scored big with their support. She would be leaving if she got this scholarship, but they weren't upset, not even Doc Julian was mad about it.

After work, she told Noah about the interview. He was happy but seemed distracted. She Read more about Professor Dunwitty and his career while Noah worked. That night, Noah held her close, not even attempting to make love. She worried, but she guessed he was exhausted, or she seemed tired. She didn't like the distance but didn't know how to change it.

On Friday afternoon after she switched into a dress, Sharron drove her to the campus and let her out right in front of the art building. She went in and sat by the offices, waiting until her appointment. The door opened, and it seemed like Dunwitty really liked the previous candidate. She couldn't help but be nervous. If she didn't get this scholarship, it would take years to finish her course work.

"Miss Anderson, come in, come in," Dunwitty said.

A woman stepped close and shook her hand the second she walked into the room. "I'm Lila, and it's a pleasure to meet you. We have the full panel set up, and we're ready to go."

She shook Lila's hand then turned to follow Professor Dunwitty into a large room. There were three paintings on easels. She went to the first one, squinting as she studied the painting. After a few seconds, she turned and looked at the people sitting at a table.

"Hello, I'm Keeley Anderson."

"Miss, Anderson, I'm Professor Fisher," a tall woman in a brown dress said. "I noticed you went to that one painting and stared at it. Why?"

She moved back to the painting and turned on the flashlight on her phone. "It looks like an original Monet. It's not."

"How do you know?" Professor Fisher asked.

She turned to the woman and gave a quick smile, praying she wasn't making a fool of herself. "All three of the paintings are amazing. They are beautiful. The first, a Picasso. I believe it's an original. You can tell by the colors, the canvas, and the frame. The second painting is from Georgia O'Keeffe. Her work redefined what art in America is. Then there is this painting. It's beautiful and an excellent forgery."

The man she didn't know stood and moved to her. "I'm Professor Newman, how do you know it's a fake?"

"The color blue isn't right. It's too blue. Also, the strokes, they aren't as sure and solid as what Monet used.

This painting has a lot of photos of it. People love it and love its fame. However, that means a forgery is going to be good. It's almost perfect, but it's not exact."

Professor Dunwitty clapped. "Good job. Wow, no one else has even noticed. See, I told you she is brilliant."

Professor Newman reached out to shake her hand. "Congratulations."

"Thank you. It really is an easy spot, though. Had it been another artist, I might have gotten it wrong."

"Oh, I meant congratulations on getting the scholarship." Professor Newman's eyes twinkled as he shot her a huge smile. "I can't wait to get you in a class. Now then, Dunwitty said you were thinking of doing masters."

Shock filled her. "Um, yes, I'd like to work in a museum one day." Had she just received a scholarship?

"Ah, yes. I love museum work. You'll need a supervisor—"

"Newman, don't rush the girl," Dunwitty said.

"Precisely." Professor Fisher took her arm and led her to the table. "She may prefer to have me as an advisor. But really, it depends on her focus. Isn't that right, Dunwitty?"

"Yes, yes."

They all settled into their seats. She stumbled over and sat down, staring at the group. Her hands were shaking. Had she really just won a scholarship for school?

"I'm stumped," she said as she stared at the trio.

"Why," Dunwitty asked. "Because you came in and solved the one problem we needed solved, and you didn't have to be prompted."

She nodded. "Yes, I just can't believe I...are you sure?"

"Yes, young lady. You are exactly the type of student we want. Please ask questions, challenging thinking, amaze us with facts. We love it." Dunwitty's smile stretched wide. "You are the type of student we need."

"Thank you. Thank you so much. I think I have every-thing turned in to the university." She went through her list, trying to come up with what else needed to be done.

"We have papers you'll need to sign once we write up the last of the information," Dunwitty said. "Really, it's not much. You'll be attending starting in August. The course load is difficult, but I believe you'll be able to keep up."

Excitement filled her. She'd loved Columbia, but that time was over. Now she had a new adventure, and she couldn't wait to get back into classes. Her stomach twisted. She'd have to leave Doc Julian's office. The staff had been so supportive and kind. She hoped they understood.

"You've gone quiet," Professor Fisher said. "Does the coursework scare you?"

"No, not exactly. I mean, I'm overwhelmed. I didn't want to get my hopes up. I work with nice people who have supported me through difficult times. I was thinking about leaving the office. It will be sad, but this is a chance of a lifetime."

Fisher nodded. "It is. A scholarship like this one is hard to get. You had a lot of tough competition."

She swallowed over the lump in her throat. "Thank you for giving me this chance."

Dunwitty straightened, his face serious. "This will be tough. We expect a lot from you."

"Hopefully, I'll deliver more than you expect." She looked at them each in the eye before saying more. "This is my future, and I'm not playing with it."

After more congratulations, a tour of the art building, signing some papers, and a visit to the registrar's office, she stepped outside and called Noah.

"Hey, I'm in the parking lot," Noah said before she could say anything.

"Which one?" She looked around, not seeing his car.

He chuckled. "You would ask that. This campus is big. Tell me where you are, and I'll drive over."

"I can walk to you," she offered.

"Nope. It's getting dark. I wouldn't feel right with you walking across campus. Just stay there, I'll come to you. I messed up and went to where we started the tour. You're at the art building, aren't you?"

"Yes. It's off Key Circle. It's the Fine Arts building. But it's not a far walk."

"No, just give me a moment. I'm already driving. I have the directions punched into my mapping software. Don't worry. I'll be there in like two minutes. I'm already on Bauerle Road."

She laughed as he talked. He was describing each tree or grouping of trees along the path.

"I'm at the stop sign now."

"I see the lights of your car."

"Good, now you can tell me how everything went. I want to hear it all. When will you know?"

She was having a hard time keeping it from him. Her excitement bubbled up. This really was happening. She prayed he didn't take back his offer to have her live with him.

The car stopped in front of her, and she pulled open the door. Noah had opened his door, but she was too fast and was already sitting next to him. He shut his door then leaned over and pulled her close. His lips brushed over hers, and she sighed.

"How did it go?" Noah asked.

She felt like she was vibrating. Happiness spilled out,

SEARCHING FOR KEELEY   179

and Noah returned her wide smile. There was no way she'd ever be able to play anything cool and hold back information.

"Oh my God." She squeezed his arm. "Noah, I got it. I mean, I really got it. Like they told me tonight that I got the full scholarship."

"What?" Surprise shown on his face.

"Yes, I got it. I'm going back to school."

"Wow. Congratulations."

He pulled her into a kiss that filled her with joy. She had a man who was kind and loving, and she would be going back to school to study for her dream job.

Noah pulled away, his smile wide. "I'm so impressed. That is awesome. We should celebrate."

"Let's order pizza." She was on top of the world. This could change everything.

Noah kissed her again then turned to put the car in gear. He eased away from the curb while she strapped in.

"I was serious about you moving in. I want you to be able to accomplish your dreams."

She hugged her bag, thinking this could just be the best time in her life. Everything was working out in her favor. Soon she would be back and school, working toward her dream, all while living with an awesome man who made her life exceptional. If only the issue with the abduction would get settled then everything would be perfect. She couldn't think about that now, it was time to celebrate. For all she knew the man who wanted her had moved on. There wasn't any way he would come after her, not now.

CHAPTER TWENTY-ONE

MOVING IN WITH NOAH HAD GONE SMOOTHLY. SHE was still working at Doc Julian's office for another two days. School would start in two weeks and her last day was on Friday.

Living with Noah had been so much easier than she'd believed. He was calm and didn't freak out when she was worried about things that happened. She'd be upset about how to get her books when she got off work too late and felt like she'd never be able to get to the school and pick them up. Then Noah would have a calm solution.

She was on her way home from work. Sharron had driven her to the grocery store two blocks away from Noah's place. She didn't want to tell Noah she walked the two blocks home. Instead, she'd assured him Sharron dropped her off right at the apartment. It had been over a month since she'd been taken. The cops had Mitchell, and there wasn't any reason to think the old man would come after her. He was probably in Mexico and would never come back to the united states.

The weather wasn't too bad. Sure it was hot, but everywhere was hot, even in Sharron's car since it had been sitting in the sun all day.

Her phone rang. Noah's name flash on the display. Happiness filled her as she answered. "Hey, when do you get off?"

"I'm off now. Are you almost home? Why do I hear road noise?"

"I'm close. Sharron was going to the store so I had her drop me at the store."

"Wait, you're walking?" Panic filled his voice.

"I'm fine." She didn't want him to worry.

She heard the car ding and then the engine start. "I'm coming to get you."

She let go of a heavy sigh. "You really don't have to."

"It's still not safe." Worry filled his voice.

"When will it ever be safe?"

"I don't know, but it's not now."

She huffed out a breath. "I'm close."

"Where are you?"

She glanced over to the shops that were far away at the front of the alley, cringing at the thought of revealing exactly where she was. It was faster to walk behind the store and cut through the alley. There were fewer people, but that hadn't bugged her until Noah had called and sounded all worried. "Next to the alley by the store."

"Good lord. I'll be there in a moment."

She could hear Noah muttering about traffic, and she snorted. "I'm fine." She smiled as a car that looked similar to Noah's pulled in at the end of the alley. "That's your car in the alley, right?"

"No. I'm still a block away," his voice rose to almost screaming.

Her breath caught with panic. "Oh, it looks like your car. They're stopping."

"Keeley, turn around and go to the grocery store."

She spun, taking off at a fast clip toward the front of the store. She glanced back and saw the car was moving fast. Then she spied Noah's car in the lot, heading her way, but he was still too far away. She raced out of the alley and up beside the store. The other car, the one behind her, was too close and Noah wasn't close enough.

The strange car zoomed up right beside her and slammed on the breaks, blocking her from moving forward. She jumped back and stumbled but stayed upright. The door to the passenger compartment opened.

Noah was out of his car, his gun drawn. But the man beside her already had his gun out. He didn't even give Noah a chance to say anything. The man fired and Noah dropped to the ground.

"No!" Keeley screamed.

The guy's hand wrapped around her arm, and he tugged her close. "You're coming with me."

She struggled, but it was no use. The man's hold was too tight. The last thing she saw before she was shoved into the car was Noah on the ground, blood pooling around him. Her heart shattered as she was pushed into the back of the vehicle. Her man was going to die because she'd been stupid. Why hadn't she waited for Noah or insisted Sharron drop her at home? She'd assumed no one was after her. Now she was trapped in the back of a car, her man was lying in a pool of blood, and there was no escape.

She couldn't allow them to take her far. If she didn't get away, she'd be dead. Keeley gathered her strength and started kicking and hitting the man. At first, she was winning. Then he punched her in the head. Darkness took over as everything went dim.

Her eyes blinked open and the first thing she noticed was the road noise, then she heard talking. Her head ached, and her mouth felt like she'd swallowed sand.

Not wanting to attract attention, she closed her eyes and fought to gain some sort of sense about what was going on. The car was moving fast, so they had to be on a freeway. If she tried to jump out, she would be dead. There wasn't any way she would escape.

The men were discussing when they would get to their final destination. From what she could gather, they were taking her to an airfield. They were going to take her out of the country.

She had to fight to break free, but she was trapped in a speeding car with no way of escape. She prayed for help, prayed for someone to rescue her. Her chances for escape were dim, and rescue was even less.

The car slowed, and the road noise changed. She would have to try to break free once they stopped.

Eventually they rolled to a full stop. The car doors opened. She flashed open her eyes, seeing the man who'd been sitting beside her crawling from the car. She moved, shoving him hard. He stumbled a few steps but didn't fall.

Keeley scrambled from the car and ran about two steps before she was knocked to her knees as an explosion of pain hit. She was face down in the dirt, her body twitching when someone moved close.

"She's feisty," a man off to her left said.

"You'll have fun," the guy from the car said as he tugged her to standing. His grip was unforgiving. "Keep her locked up though, she can't be trusted."

"Oh, I intend on keeping her in a cage. She won't have freedom for years."

Keeley blinked at the man dressed in a suit and tie. He looked like an ordinary businessman, maybe better dressed than some, but normal. His dark hair was cut short, his skin tanned, and his teeth were white. He didn't seem like an evil monster, but that's what he was.

"How will you break her in?" the guy from the car asked.

"Like a horse. She'll learn to mind or be beaten. Food is also a motivator. If she wants to eat, she'll have to obey. I paid a lot of money for her and I'm not willing to give her up."

The man moved to stand in front of her. His eyes appraised her like she was food or a shirt, not a human. She gathered spit in her mouth and let it fly. The wad of spittle landed on the man's cheek.

He pulled out a white napkin and wiped his face. Keeley expected him to retaliate, but he didn't hit her. She almost wanted the violence. If she could force him to react, force him to hurt her, maybe her pain and suffering would be less. She would die, and it would be over.

The thought brought a shiver to her. She didn't really want to die, but she didn't want to be this man's caged sex toy.

"You're going to allow her to get away with that?" the guy holding her asked.

The man in the suit held her gaze. "Oh, don't worry, she'll pay. Every day for the rest of her life, she'll pay. There won't be one day that she enjoys anything. Trust me, I have plans for her that would make even you cry." The man in the suit turned away but spun back to them. "Put her in the dog kennel located in the cargo hold. Dogs don't get to sit with humans."

Keeley swallowed over her fear. She didn't think it was safe to ride in the cargo hold of an airplane. What if she froze or died? But wasn't that what she wanted?

"Come on." The guy holding her arm tugged her closer to the plane.

She struggled against his grip, but he only held on tighter. If they got her to the next location, she would be dead. There wasn't any way she would survive this man. He was evil.

The man holding her let go then hit her with a shock. She dropped to the ground, her body still buzzing. When the pain lessened, she blinked up at him and saw him holding a long stick. They were using a cattle prod to control her.

She was dragged the rest of the way and shoved into the dog kennel. The gate on the kennel was closed and locked with a keyed padlock. Tears sprang to her eyes. Her life was over. She would never become an art historian. She'd never work in a museum. Her life with Noah was gone, all because she'd walked behind the grocery store, going the shortcut, instead of just staying in the store and waiting until Noah came to pick her up. Why hadn't she waited? The air in her lungs seemed to be failing. Maybe she would suffocate in here.

CHAPTER TWENTY-TWO

Pain filled Noah when he came to. His arm was on fire, and his head split with pain, but he had to find Keeley.

The squeal of tires wasn't far away. He stood on shaky legs and turned, seeing the car that had Keeley screech to a halt at the end of the lot.

Maybe there was hope. He struggled with his door but got it open and hopped into his car. Driving wasn't comfortable, but he was able to manage to get out of the lot and was about five, maybe ten cars behind the one holding Keeley. She had to be frightened.

Noah dialed Long, not giving her a chance to say anything before he began speaking. "They have Keeley. I've been shot."

"What? Where are you?"

"Following. We're getting on I 1 0 and heading north."

"Crap, how bad are you?"

"I'm good enough to drive."

"Give me a moment," Long said.

"We're about to pass Camp Bullis Road."

"Stay on the line," Long shouted.

Noah kept the car in his sights. He couldn't lose Keeley. His arm hurt like a bitch, but he was still able to use it. The pain must have just wiped him out for a few seconds. He didn't want to look at the wound because he feared it would look worse and make him queasy. There weren't any options, he had to stay with Keeley.

"Noah, you still there?"

"Yes, ma'am. I'm sticking with her. We passed state road 3351."

"Where could they be going?" Long asked.

"No clue, but I'm not giving up on her."

"Where did you get shot?"

"My arm. Thank goodness my car isn't a manual transmission."

"I have a team here. We're looking at why they are headed that way. They could be going to El Paso and over the border, but it's doubtful. Or they could be driving to another state."

The car wasn't speeding, and he had to fight the urge to race up behind them. He didn't want to tip them off that he was back here. The last thing he needed was that car to crash and to have Keeley killed in the crash.

"You still there, Noah."

"Yeah, yeah. The pain is a bit much, but I'm here."

"We have a helicopter in the air and Cody is driving that way. He's about five miles behind you."

Noah prayed they could catch up. He was about to freak out when the car up ahead turned on its blinker.

"Oh God, they are taking an exit."

"Which one?"

"Um," he watched and pulled to the right, not signaling

as he slowed even more to take the exit. "He took Fair Oaks, exit 546."

"There's an airport out there. He's going to the airport," Long said.

"Shit, how big? Could they have flown in a private jet?"

Long was talking to someone beside her. Noah followed the car, staying back enough to make it look like he wasn't going to turn after them. Though they were making a left, Noah moved to the right-hand lane and turned on his blinker. The people in the car must not have been paying attention to him at all because they didn't slow or speed up when he moved over and made a left.

"They made a left on Fair Oaks," Noah said.

"Shit," Long said.

Panic filled him. "What?"

"The airfield is big enough for a private jet. This guy could go almost anywhere. If they take off, we're shit out of luck."

"Where is their air traffic control?"

"Give me a minute," Long barked.

"She doesn't have but a minute." Desperation filled him. He didn't want to lose her. She was his one, the only one he wanted to make a life with.

He could hear Long speaking to someone. This sucked so badly. He just wanted Keeley to be safe. His whole future was wrapped up in Keeley. Even if they didn't last, he couldn't allow someone to do this to her.

"Agent Long, are you—"

"I'm here. We are talking to air traffic control. They are going to close the airport due to the weather or something. They'll delay the plane as long as they can. Our helicopter should land there in the next five minutes. And Cody's group just took the exit. They are close. Hang tight."

The other car had slipped through the gate. There was no one here watching the gate, so the guy must have been relatively confident they hadn't been followed. He saw the jet sitting off the runway. He imagined the guy had paid a large sum of money.

His phone rang and he answered. "It's Cody, where are you?"

"I was able to get through the gate but it's closed now. You'll have to run up to meet me. I'm parking and getting out of my car."

He'd turned off the interior light earlier along with the headlights when he'd entered the airfield. Pain shot up his arm as he opened the door. This was the most important operation he'd ever been involved in. Keeley's life depended on him getting this right.

He made his way closer to the car where it had stopped. Keeley was standing there in front of a man in a suit. He looked like a total dick. Had she just spit in the guy's face?

"We're on property," Cody said in his ear.

He grunted and moved closer. Keeley was hauled away and taken to the plane. The man with her hit her with something that made her drop to the ground.

"Easy, Noah," Cody said. "Just let us do the dirty work here."

"Fuck." Noah watched as she was carried up a ladder and loaded into something in the side of the plane. They weren't even going to allow her to sit in the plane. She would ride in the side compartment like an animal or piece of luggage.

"Everyone in position?" Cody asked.

"What are you all doing?"

"We're going to close in," Cody said. "There are only

four of them, maybe five. We have ten not including you. Once we go, you move in and get Keeley."

"Got it." Noah swallowed over the lump in his throat. This could all go wrong, or it could go perfect. He prayed it was the second one because he really needed Keeley to survive.

CHAPTER TWENTY-THREE

Tears fell as the asshole secured the door of the cage and shut the side of the airplane, locking her in. She was going to die. Humiliation washed over her, and she cried out, praying for someone to rescue her. Noah had been shot. He was probably dead. She would never see him again. Her life was over. This was the end for her. Tears spilled down her cheeks as she held her knees close and rocked.

A loud bang was followed by people shouting. Was that shooting? Were people shooting at each other?

Her heart sped up as tears spilled down her face. What was going on? Who was shooting at who? There was more shouting, and then the hum of the engine changed. Had it just been cut off?

"Help," she cried out in a weak voice. Fear still made her voice shake and kept her from yelling louder. It was like she was trapped in a nightmare and couldn't call for help. Then she tried again. "Help."

The compartment she was locked in sprung open. Noah was right there, his smile wide.

"Oh God." She reached through the wires of the cage and tried to touch him, but she couldn't get her hand through.

"You're alive," Noah said.

A sob escaped her lips. "I thought you died."

"Hey, Noah, let me up there, and I'll help her down."

Keeley looked over and saw another guy standing near the plane.

Noah held up one finger. "I'll be here." Noah stepped away, and the other man came close.

"I don't know if you remember me. I'm Cody Whittaker. I hope you are okay."

"I've been better."

"Let's get you out of this," Cody said. "I'm guessing you don't have the key?"

"No, sir. I don't have the key."

Cody flashed her a smile and moved down two steps before he shouted. "I need bolt cutters."

"You got it," the call came across the airfield."

Cody was back by her side, wire cutters in hand. He cut the padlock securing the door to the kennel. It swung open, granting her freedom. She climbed out, and Cody helped her down. Noah was there. He pulled her to him, his lips on hers. They stayed like that for over a minute, neither of them willing to let go.

"Hey, Noah, Keeley, the ambulance is here. You both need to get checked."

"I'm fine," Keeley said. "Noah was the one shot."

"I'm okay," Noah said.

She was holding Noah up and knew he wasn't okay. When the paramedics came over, she insisted they work on him first. Once they knew he'd been shot, they agreed. This was the second time she'd been rescued and rushed to the hospital. She didn't like the trend.

After the doctor saw her and declared her okay to travel home, she went to Noah's bedside and sat with him. He hadn't needed surgery, but he had been given an IV. His eyes were closed, and she thought he was asleep. When she sat down. He opened his eyes and met her gaze.

"I thought I'd lost you." Noah reached out with his good hand, and she took it, weaving her fingers with his. She kissed each knuckle then met his gaze.

"I was so worried about you."

"Same here. I wasn't sure if you would survive."

Tears ran down her cheeks. Noah had tears in his eyes too. She lowered and brushed her lips over his. Emotions filled her so full she almost burst.

"I'm going to be fine," Noah said.

"I know I'm just happy."

"Same here. So you're still living with me, right?"

"Oh yeah, there's no way you're getting rid of me that easily." She laughed as tears slid down her cheeks. She really was happy. Noah was the love of her life, and she never wanted to lose him.

Noah was released from the hospital and Cody, along with other agents, helped them get home. After a long nap, they were alone, sitting on the couch, staring out at the moonlit apartment common area, listening to birds squawk as they sat in stillness.

"This is so peaceful," Noah said.

"It is." His phone buzzed, and Keeley grabbed it off the table and handed it to him. "Looks like Cody."

"He wants to stop by."

She nodded, knowing they would have to let others in eventually. "Sure."

There was a knock on the door, and she got up, checking the peephole before letting Cody in. He shook her hand and pulled her into a hug before moving to the couch and squeezing Noah's shoulder.

Cody leaned forward, his forearms resting on his knees. "Hey, so how are you doing?"

"I'm good. It hurts a little, but luckily it's only a bit of skin and meat missing, no bone."

"While you were driving out to that airport, the San Antonio PD did a raid on a building. Amos was there. They recovered his computer. We have the list. They're working with us. We're going to be able to take down a lot of people with this list."

Keeley sat forward, hope filling her. "Wow."

"So the man who purchased Keeley, he's in custody?" Noah asked. "And then the leader of the human trafficking ring is in jail too?"

Cody nodded. "The man who paid for Keeley is rich. Like, own a country rich. It will be hard to keep him in jail if all we had was Keeley's case."

"That's not right." Anger flashed in Keeley.

"Right or not," Cody said. "It's how it is. The justice system doesn't always bring justice. That's why we gather as much evidence as we can. His house was raided. There was a woman chained up in his basement. She was thrilled to be rescued. She's been missing for ten years. Her family is ecstatic that she's coming home. They brought in cadaver dogs. They've found at least one body, possibly more."

Keeley gasped. Noah pulled her close and hugged her. Tears filled her eyes. She couldn't help but cry. The man who wanted her was a killer. She would have eventually filled a grave on his property, she knew it.

Cody reached out and took her hand. "The man is not a

SEARCHING FOR KEELEY   195

good person. The dead bodies will keep him in jail. Keeley, you're a fighter. You survived him. Other women didn't. You fought back and won. I'm glad you were able to stay ahead of him and win."

She choked on a sob. Noah held her close, his touch soothing. She had been so close to a fate worse than death but had survived. Now she would have more than just life to live for, she had the man of her dreams who had encouraged her to go after her dreams.

"Thank you for coming by to tell us," Noah said.

"Hey, brother, that's why we're here. You know that."

"I do, but it's never been so obvious how much our updates help. I've gone to families after we've finished with the case and given updates. They are always so thankful, now I know why."

Keeley let go of Noah and stood. Cody stood, and she gave him a hug. "Thank you," she choked out on a sob.

Noah was right there, his one good arm around her. This was why Noah put in the long hours. He saved people, helped families, and made the world better. She'd been saved by him. If he hadn't come after her and stopped the asshole who had placed her in the dog kennel in the belly of that plane, she would be lost forever.

Cody stepped back and headed to the door. "I'm going to let you two get some rest. Noah, I'll see you in the morning?"

"I'll be there. I may need extra coffee, but I'll be there, ready to work on the next case."

Cody nodded and waved before stepping outside. Keeley turned to him and held out her hand. He moved close, love shining in his eyes.

"I almost lost everything."

Noah nodded, then kissed her forehead. "I almost lost you."

Keeley leaned back and looked him in the eyes. "I love you."

His lips curved up in a broad smile. "I love you too. Maybe all of this pushed us together more quickly than if it hadn't happened, but Keeley, I want you as mine forever. I love you. I never want to lose you."

She wrapped her arms around his waist and held him close, knowing that from here on out, her life would be filled with wonder and magic. There may be some hard times to come, and she and Noah would have to learn what living together really meant, but she was ready for whatever came their way.

Noah leaned back and met her gaze. "There's no one else in this world I'd rather have my life with."

Her heart filled with even more love. "Same for me, love. Same for me."

Noah leaned in, grunting when she brushed up against his injured arm. She sucked in air and was about to apologize, but his lips landed on hers. Their kiss may not have been the sexiest or the smoothest, but she had love from Noah, and that was all that mattered.

The End

ABOUT JULIA BRIGHT

Julia Bright is the author of the contemporary military romance Dark Eagle series, and is an Operation Alpha Author. Julia lives in the south where "bless your heart" is an insult and "shut up" shows love. Julia has been reading since she could open a book and has taken her passion for words and combined it with her love of travel to create stories full of passion and excitement. If you love a good book with a fantastic happily ever after, you'll enjoy a Julia Bright novel. For a dash of paranormal romance and urban fantasy, pick up a JS Bright book.

ALSO BY JULIA BRIGHT

Seeking Justice

Justice for Amber - Also a part of Susan Stoker's World

Dark Eagle Series

Survive The Fall

Live Past The Edge

Hold on Through The Pain

In Susan Stoker's World

Saving Lorelei

Rescuing Amy

Saving Sloan

Fated Forever

Mine to Claim

Mine to Love

Spellcasting & Demon Magic

Strange Magic - Hunted in Darkness

Hunted in Light

Made in the USA
Columbia, SC
18 April 2023

15494253R10124